THEIR CONQUERED BRIDE

A BRIDGEWATER MÉNAGE

GRACE GOODWIN

GET A FREE BOOK!

JOIN MY MAILING LIST TO BE THE FIRST TO KNOW OF NEW RELEASES, FREE BOOKS, SPECIAL PRICES AND OTHER AUTHOR GIVEAWAYS.

http://freescifiromance.com

lizabeth

I LEANED my elbows on the dried wood railing on the small balcony of our second floor hotel room and sighed. The dark night did nothing to hide a woman's cries coming from the room next door. I should have been sound asleep hours ago, blissfully unaware at this time of night, except I was restless and worried. Soon I would no longer be Miss Elizabeth Lewis. No, in two short days I would meet my new husband, Mr. Samuel Jenkins, and pray that he looked upon me with favor. A bit of desire would be nice as well.

When a woman's soft calls reached my ears, I tossed back the tangled covers and followed the noises outside to peek into the next room, worried that the cries she made were caused by pain. As my bare feet pressed to the wooden planks under me, the unmistakable sounds of carnal pleasure reached my ears.

She wasn't in pain, at least not the kind she might want to escape.

I would not look.

I would not look.

Damn it. I looked, and clenched my legs together at the scene playing out. This woman was most definitely *not* being harmed. With their balcony door wide open to take in the warm night air and the candles lit on the small nightstand, I could easily see into their room.

On the bed, a woman was on her hands and knees being fucked from behind, her long dark hair swinging in a wild braid over her shoulder, half of it loose and falling. While I was a virgin, I knew exactly what the word fucking meant; I'd just never seen people doing it.

My first thought was that she was a prostitute, for surely no decent woman would be so eager or willing, so dirty. I had spent many sleepless nights imagining fucking. I'd thought the woman would be on her back, legs spread, but this... oh my! My imagination had not done it justice, for I had expected the act to occur between a woman and a man, not a woman and *two* men! Two! The shock of this vision was so carnal and wicked that my pussy clenched beneath my nightgown and I couldn't look away. I didn't want to.

The animalistic sounds escaping from the woman's throat made me bite my lip and hold back a moan of my own. My heart skipped a beat as the woman's cries of encouragement reached me.

"God, do it, Xander. Do it. Fuck me harder. Fill me

up." The woman was a dark-haired beauty, lush and curvy, just like me, which was a curse because it wasn't difficult to imagine myself there, between the two handsome men, begging to be taken and used, begging for more. The man behind her, Xander, had dark hair and a rugged beard. He was pure muscle, his firm grip on her hips nearly lifting the woman off the bed, her breasts swaying, with each hard thrust as he plundered her with his hard cock. I watched as the thick length disappeared inside her pussy over and over, coated and glistening with her wet welcome. He wasn't gentle with her, just as she'd begged.

"Fuck, Tyler, she's so tight. Do you think she's ready to take both of us?" Xander asked, his voice dark and rough. I watched, mesmerized by the way the taut muscles in his buttocks and lower back flexed every time he pushed inside her. Xander was stockier, with a massive chest and muscled body I longed to touch. It was his thick cock that had me mesmerized, easily the size of my wrist. My own pussy clenched at the thought of being breached by something so massive.

Where Xander was dark, Tyler was fair and beautiful as he knelt in front of the woman, his long cock jutting from the light-colored nest of curls between his bent legs. She stroked him with her hand, from the thick base to the flared crown. I wanted to be that woman, taken by one dark angel and one light. A striking contrast.

It wasn't just the sound of Xander's hips slapping her bare bottom with each stroke, or the wet, slippery sounds of fucking that made me shiver in the night, unable to move, unable to look away. No, it was her face, her moans and gasps as he struck her bare bottom with his hand. Hard. He was spanking her!

"Please. Please. Please." Her breathy requests were timed to the deep plunge of the giant cock into her pussy and I reached down over my gown to touch myself there, in the forbidden place, in the one place I was taught never, ever to touch.

"Emily, you know better," Xander warned. "I tell you when to come. I say when, love, or you will be punished." He spanked her again as he pulled back, then drove home. She groaned in response as the skin on her bottom turned a dark shade of pink. "You're going to take us both, sweetheart. You love when Tyler's in your pussy while I fuck that snug ass."

Tyler waited for Xander's nod before shifting position to lie flat on his back on the bed, his cock rising from his body like a sword, a weapon. He caught the woman by her long dark hair and I imagined that hard pull on my scalp, used my free hand to pull on my own hair just as he tugged on hers and he issued his first command. "Crawl over the bed and ride me, baby. Now."

Emily whimpered, but it was because as she moved, Xander slipped from her. I could see her pussy open and wet, red and swollen. Well used and yet they weren't done. Xander's fingers slid through her wetness to touch her back entrance and I bit my lip as I noticed the tip of his finger disappearing inside her. I saw the forbidden hole glistening as Xander painted it with her desire.

Tyler smiled and pulled harder on her hair, so I pulled on my own, my hand over my own sensitive nub speeding up to match the rhythm of Xander's hands stroking her from ass to pussy as she pulled away from him. She stopped halfway to her destination and pulled back, yanking away from the hand in her hair to shove her wet pussy against Xander as he fucked her with his fingers. "Please."

Xander laughed and struck her bare bottom so hard I could see another handprint from the balcony, the pink sting on her naked flesh. "You're not in control, sweetheart. Tsk, tsk. You should know better. I decide when to fuck you. I decide how wide to spread that pretty little ass." He spanked her again and she moaned, leaning down to rub her hard nipples along Tyler's hard, hairy thighs. "Now, get up there and ride Tyler's cock like a good girl. Let him feel how hot and wet you are."

She scrambled to do as instructed and eagerly sank onto Tyler's cock until the cheeks of her bottom were spread so wide across his hips that I could see the tight rose of her backside. She leaned over and captured her lover's lips in a hot duel of tongues as Xander crawled onto the bed and settled behind her. He pulled and tugged on her bottom, spreading her open until I could see the soft, glistening pink of her wet pussy stretched around the base of Tyler's cock. He spanked her ass again, over and over as she moaned and cried out, most of her cries buried in a deep and thorough kiss.

I rubbed my own tender flesh faster and harder, desperate to be filled with something to ease the ache, but I knew that would be too much to explain away should my sisters wake from where they slept in the bed behind me. A hand outside my gown I could explain away, but my nightgown up around my hips and my own fingers deep inside my wet pussy? Well, that one would mark me as the dirty, naughty girl my uncle had accused me of being.

God help me, he was right. I was unclean. Disgusting. No pure woman should feel wet heat sliding down her thighs simply from watching another woman, most likely a prostitute, enjoying two men.

Hell, no decent woman should watch this at all, but I wasn't decent. I was broken. Damaged goods. My mother's passionate nature was in my blood. I'd been corrupted by evil since before my birth and had never been able to recover no matter how hard I tried.

And I did try. I spent countless hours on my knees, begging the good Lord to take away my sinful thoughts, my lustful body, the ache between my thighs that longed to be touched. But he never answered my prayers.

I ached. I wanted. *I lusted.*

So when Tyler pulled and tugged on the woman's nipples, I tugged on my own, mimicking his movements exactly. Xander rubbed some kind of oil over her back entrance and, using his thick thumb, worked it deep inside her. I moaned, then held my breath, hoping I hadn't just given myself away.

No. The woman made noise of her own, more than covering for my lapse of control.

As Xander aligned his thick cock behind her, I shuddered. I had never imagined this. Not in a hundred thousand years would I have ever imagined something so wicked. I should look away. I should go back into my room and curl up on the floor next to my sisters' bed and sleep.

I should at least try to save my soul, but just as my

uncle had accused me, I was corrupted because I could not tear my eyes away from the sight of Xander's giant cock beginning to stretch her forbidden place wider and wider.

Emily panted and gasped as he entered her slowly, Tyler still balls deep in her pussy, still playing with her hard nipples, still pulling on her hair.

I shuddered as my hand moved faster and faster. I wanted to feel it all, but I only had two hands, and one of them had to be on my clit.

The two men moved opposite one another, one filling her pussy as the other pulled out of her bottom, then reversing course.

She begged them to go faster. Begged them to let her come, but all her words earned her was another hard spanking and a reprimand from the dark-haired Adonis behind her. "You don't come until I give you permission."

"Yes, sir. Please. Please. I can't wait anymore."

The men glanced at each other—they worked in perfect harmony to give the woman pleasure—and Tyler, buried in her wet pussy, slid his hand first to her hip, which made her beg him to hurry, then between their bodies to the sensitive flesh on a woman's body. I, too, stroked the same place beneath my gown.

The dominant one, Xander, fucked her harder and faster in her ass as Tyler worked her clit and pulled her hair, hard, arching her back and neck up toward the ceiling, opening her for their possession. They were thorough lovers, but still gentle with her. They watched her closely to ensure her pleasure, to ensure she was loving everything they were doing. "We know how you like it. Hard and deep. Isn't that right, baby?"

"Yes, sir. Please!"

"Arch your back. Get your ass in the air. We'll give you what you need."

She was shaking now, sweat dripping down her temples to roll down her neck to her breasts. Tyler licked it from her skin and I shuddered nearly as much as the woman who enjoyed the harsh rasp of his tongue.

With a grunt, Xander struck her bare bottom hard, over and over as she bucked and whimpered. I couldn't imagine her liking how rough they were with her, but she did. She was wild as she was completely taken by both of them.

Finally, Xander set her free.

"Come now. Come all over us."

It was like he was talking to me.

I shattered, right there on the balcony, my release rushing over me as the woman found hers.

It was the most erotic thing I'd ever done. The dirtiest. As my pussy convulsed and my body quaked, out of control, I kept my eyes squarely on the trio, watched the slide of wet cock in and out of her pussy, the hard thrust of the other in her bottom, and I envied her.

I wanted that, even a man's cock in my bottom. Not some dirty old miner more than twice my age. I wanted a young man desperate to take me, to make me his. I wanted raw animal passion and a man who would make me shatter into a thousand pieces from pleasure.

I was jealous of a prostitute, and that proved once and for all that my uncle was right to send me away. He was right to disown me. I was dirty, my thoughts unclean. I was a bad, bad girl. No matter how hard I tried, I couldn't stop.

Mr. Jenkins was my future, my soon-to-be husband. He would lay with me and make me his. I could hope there was passion in our bed. I did hope. I hoped he filled me with his cock and made me lose control, made me beg for release. And if not, then I had what I'd just seen to keep me warm on cold nights.

Tomorrow the stage would take me to Hayes where I would I start my new life as a respected, pious, perfect wife.

Tomorrow, I would be perfect. Tonight?

Tonight I would dare to imagine myself in that room, between those two men, being fucked until I collapsed into a weak puddle on my lover's chest.

CHAPTER 2

"SHE'LL BE HERE any day now." The bastard sitting across from me at the gambling table clenched his teeth around a stub of a cigar. "My mail-order bride."

Logan and I, along with Evan, sat around the card table with the filthy old man playing poker. I caught his name when he and his two sons first sat down. Samuel Jenkins. With him were his two grown sons, Tad and Harry. The saloon was rowdy and crowded due to the afternoon's cattle drive. The cattle arrived and brought with them a bunch of men who longed for cheap whiskey and loose women.

Logan, Evan and I, along with nine other men, were just passing through this town on our way to the Bridgewater Ranch and were eager to see the town behind us. If these three Jenkins men were the kinds of folk who lived here, I didn't want to meet any more. They'd been talking nonstop, not of their bride, the innocent woman scheduled to arrive from Omaha in two days' time to marry Mr. Jenkins, Sr., but of the wedding night.

"What if she won't marry you, Pa?" The elder son looked close to my own age of thirty. He was missing his two front teeth and his lips were stained black with chewing tobacco. If possible, he smelled even worse than his father, who reeked of sweat and piss, his fingernails coated in unwashed black from working the mines.

"She'll marry me. She ain't got no choice. Ain't no going back." Jenkins slammed back his fifth shot of whiskey and I cringed for the poor, unsuspecting woman traveling to marry him.

"She'll be wed to Pa, just like we planned," the younger son said, his eyes wide with perverted glee. He had to be no older than twenty. "Come on, Tad, tell these soldier boys about the sweet pussy we're going to get."

I arched my brow at the kid's words. I wasn't in uniform, and neither were my friends, but I knew from looking around the bar that we stood out, uniform or not. We were retired from the military, our service done for a country we would most likely never see again. I, for one, was ready to get to Bridgewater and settle down with a nice warm woman. So, I understood what the old man wanted, but knew my brow creased in confusion at the younger man's words. I'd thought old man Jenkins was the one set to marry.

"Shut up, Harry. Ain't nobody's business." Tad tossed a

few coins into the center of the table. "But I hope she's got big titties."

Samuel Jenkins slapped the table and the coins jumped. "I get her *first*," he clarified, waving his hand between his sons. "And I told you, after I'm done, we'll be taking turns with her." He glanced at me, then Logan, as if to gauge our reactions. "You men ever share a woman before?"

I flicked my gaze to my friend Logan, quickly understanding the men's intentions, but his expression was unreadable. I wasn't about to tell these men anything. Logan called for another card and the old man dealt him one. Who was the poor woman arriving tomorrow? The need to warn her stirred to life inside me. No woman deserved what these men had planned for her. I needed to know the woman's name and the best way to discover information was to let the men talk.

Jenkins didn't know who he was playing cards with, for if he did, he would know that we *always* shared a woman. It was the way of our group, the dozen of us in town, plus those already settled at Bridgewater. We'd all spent time enjoying the culture and customs in Mohamir —a small Middle Eastern country where our regiment had been stationed—and were now traveling to Bridge-water where we could live our way without bothering anyone.

Our trusted friend, Whitmore Kane, had written telling us of the growing number of men settling on a ranch in the Montana Territory with their brides. He'd invited those from our regiment to join them. Two men— or more—marrying one woman, the custom of Mohamir, certainly didn't follow the strict dictates of Victorian England. Puritanical America didn't follow suit either, but based on what we'd seen of the Montana Territory, out here under the big sky, there was plenty of room to do as one wished. Even the Jenkinses believed that, but what they intended did not favor the bride in any way.

The Mohamiran marriage custom put the woman's needs first. The husbands loved her, honored her, cherished her, protected her. Possessed her body and took pride in the pleasure he gave her.

Evan broke the silence. "I'm a one-woman man myself."

That was the truth, for he—along with Daniel—would claim only one woman. Logan and I would share a bride. The others in our group, all bachelors, had already agreed to the same and now they waited for that one special woman to come along and change everything. Our way of life was nothing like what these men had planned for their future bride and the stench of the idea—and them —reeked.

Jenkins shook his head as if disappointed. "You don't know what you're missing. My boys here, they like a woman between them, but the whores upstairs—" he glanced up at the ceiling as if he could see through it to the working girls being fucked while we spoke, "—aren't that eager anymore. It was over a long, cold winter night we came up with the idea for a mail-order bride."

I wanted confirmation of their intentions. "Am I to understand you hired an agency to find brides for all three of you?"

"You talk funny," the youngest one commented.

"I'm not from the Montana Territory," I replied, as if people spoke with British accents elsewhere in the country. We didn't need to draw attention to ourselves and our accents were easily noticeable. We came halfway around the world for a quiet life. We'd all had enough trouble to last a lifetime. My closest friend, the man with whom I would share a bride with, was an orphan. Logan's father passed from a bad flu when he was only nine years old. He'd run the streets of Manchester begging for food and money, trying to help his mother survive. But she had faded away right before his eyes. After she died, he'd joined the military to start over.

When our regiment arrived in Mohamir, he'd been the first one of us to see the wisdom of their ways. Two husbands meant safety and comfort for a widow and her children. That was something Logan admired and respected about their society and I agreed.

The drunken sot sitting across from me, Harry, seemed to accept my excuse and my strange accent. He turned away from me and nodded his head at his father, seemingly content with my response. Bloody idiot.

Tad called for another card, stuck it into his hand, then said, "We didn't use no agency. A newspaper advertisement was all it took."

"And it's not *three* brides," Jenkins clarified, then pointed to himself and his sons. "Only one. Why the hell do we want three noisy women in the house when we only need one?"

I saw Logan's eyebrows go up. He leaned forward, placed his forearms on the table. "You're telling me you placed an advertisement for a bride to share? And you received a reply?"

I shifted in my seat, eager to hear the answer. If a simple advertisement would bring a willing woman to us, a woman content to marry two men instead of one, our bride problem could be easily solved. Apparently, Logan also saw the possibilities. Was this how it was done in America? I was used to arranged marriages among the upper class in England, but those matches were meant to preserve genetic lineage and station. This country broke from king and country a century before to avoid such legacies.

"She must be a hundred-year-old hag," Evan said, rolling his eyes.

Logan chuckled, but Jenkins held his hand in a fist, shaking it in Evan's face as if my friend were an idiot. "Now hold on. Of course not! She's a nice young virgin. Twenty and five. And I got her likeness right here." Jenkins dug into his jacket pocket and pulled out a thick photograph with ripped edges for Logan to see. Both Evan and I leaned forward for a glimpse of the woman, but Tad had other ideas. He ripped the photograph from his father's hand before any of us could take a look.

"Damn it, Pa. They'll try to steal her away."

Jenkins looked to Logan, who shook his head in disgust and lied through his teeth, his thick American accent as fake as the smile on his face. "I already got a wife. Why would I want yours?"

Jenkins raised an eyebrow and Tad spit a wad of black slime onto the floor near my feet as his father preened like a peacock. "She thinks she's marrying a forty-year-old widower with wee sons to take care of. And that part's true." He grinned and his eyes narrowed. "She'll be takin' care of my boys, just not in the way she thinks."

Tad chuckled and looked to his younger brother. "She'll be taking very *special* care of us with that pussy of hers."

It was a good thing I only had one shot of that rotgut whiskey, for my stomach heaved at the plan these men had devised. The father was going to marry a woman and, without her knowing, planned to share her with his two grown sons. The poor woman thought she would be getting a younger man with small children. The elder Jenkins had to be fifty if he were a day.

My own mother had been married to an old man, a man in his sixties and she just eighteen. She was the second wife of my father, the marquess of Barton. It had been a loveless marriage, a marriage solely to link two families. My mother had been a pawn, just like this Jenkins' bride. Where my mother had no power to deny her fate, this woman was choosing to become Jenkins' bride. But why? What drove a woman to marry a man sight unseen? Desperation, if I had to venture a guess.

That didn't make the situation any better.

"Taking care of you two with her pussy?" Evan pointed from Tad to Harry, his back stiff as a giant oak, but none of the Jenkins men noticed.

"It's all in the family. We'll all fuck her. Little Harry here has an itch that needs to be scratched. A virgin itch. Well, not *quite* virgin, since I'll break her in first." Jenkins winked at his youngest, *Little Harry*, who was well over six feet of solid muscle, his massive size no doubt acquired over weeks and months of moving rock in the mines.

"I doubt this woman will be too keen on the idea," I said, keeping my voice neutral despite the gut-churning desire I had to pound Jenkins' face into dust. My mother hadn't been forced to bed other men. In fact, once I was born, the heir, I doubted she bedded any man ever again.

Logan and I would share a bride someday, but it would be for *our wife's* benefit, not ours. When we claimed her, she'd be the center of our universe. We'd cherish her, love her, protect her, never do anything to defile her or betray her trust. We would be nothing like these men. If something happened to me, I was comforted to know that my future bride, and any children we might have, would be safe and cared for by Logan. I knew he felt the same.

I *was* the marquess of Barton, had been for the past five years when my father had died at the ripe age of eighty-eight. A bride didn't stay safe and warm because of a title. It was the man who'd inherited it that she needed.

Bloody fucking hell. I'd left England to avoid these kinds of shenanigans and we were in the thick of it now. None of us could walk away with the information these men were imparting. The west was a rough place. Wild. A man's world. It was hard enough for a woman to survive and no woman deserved to be preyed upon by the likes of the Jenkins men.

I didn't even need to look at Logan to know he agreed with me. Evan was having a harder time keeping his feelings in check. He tossed his cards on the table. "I fold. I need a drink."

He stood, his chair scraping across the scarred wood

floor. Glancing at me first, then at Logan, Evan shook his head. "I'll see you later."

I lifted my chin in response and the Jenkins men watched him leave.

"What's his problem?" old man Jenkins asked. He didn't wait for me to respond, only leaned forward, then looked left and right. "We're keeping it in the family. It's not like we'll let *anyone* fuck her. Any seed that fills that pussy will belong to a Jenkins."

"And her ass. You said an ass fuck is even tighter than a virgin pussy," Little Harry countered. The eagerness I saw on his face made me sick.

Tad grinned and made a crude gesture with his hands. "You two can have her pussy. I'm taking that virgin ass."

I was ready to reach across the table and punch Tad in the nose, but that wouldn't help the woman who was unaware of their intentions. While I had to agree that ass fucking was the tightest fuck ever, Logan and I would only do it after much preparation and only when the woman was so damn hot she begged us to take her completely. I doubted Tad could arouse a woman, let alone prepare her properly.

"You think the people in this town will like knowing what you're doing?" I asked.

Little Harry grinned. "We're not tellin' people. It's our secret. Ain't like she'll talk neither. Since talking would ruin her reputation and all."

Clearly, none of them could hold their whiskey for their secret was now ours. While we wouldn't go off and tell the sheriff of their perverted plans, we could certainly intervene on behalf of the woman. Once the vows were said, these men could do whatever they wanted with the bride. Beat her, share her, fuck her. She belonged to her husband in the eyes of the law and there was nothing that said he couldn't share with his sons.

"When is she expected to arrive?" Logan asked.

Ah, he was right there with me. We weren't letting these men anywhere near the woman who was coming halfway across the country with expectations of a *real* marriage. What would drive a woman to accept an advertisement for a husband, sight unseen? She had to be desperate. Alone. The more I thought about this bastard's plans, the angrier I became.

Old man Jenkins shrugged. "Day after tomorrow. Coming in on the stage from Omaha."

I raised my hand and signaled to the bartender to bring another bottle of whiskey. He brought it over quickly and I took it from him in exchange for a few coins.

"Gentlemen, this is in honor of you and your future bride." I filled their shot glasses to the brim as I choked out the words.

Little Harry whooped as old man Jenkins reached across and slapped Logan on the shoulder. "I'd say you're welcome to stop by later in the week and partake of our bride." He winked. "But she'll already be more than busy enough riding three cocks."

They lifted their glasses and tossed the bitter brew back. I refilled again and again as we played cards for the next few hours, ensuring the bottle was empty and none of them would be conscious tomorrow morning when Logan and I headed out of town to intercept that stage.

CHAPTER 3

 *lizabeth*

As the coach pulled to a stop after hours of rocking and swaying, I was eager for a hotel room and a bath. My back ached nearly as much as my bottom, and I knew when I lay down to sleep later, the world would still feel as if it moved beneath me.

But, we had arrived. Finally! My sisters and I were hundreds of miles away from my vile uncle. I would meet my husband and my sisters and I would be safe. Protected. For once in my life, I would be taken care of by a man who wanted me.

I needed a bath, but I wouldn't be choosy. I'd settle for a basin and ewer with fresh water to rid me of the miles of travel dust. I'd seen the never-ending open prairie, the tall grass turning toward gold. Hayes was much smaller than Omaha, and the first thing we couldn't miss on the edge of town was a church, the sacred house of worship where I would soon take my solemn vows.

A schoolhouse stood guard over a yard full of a dozen playing children and a long row of shops and houses lined the main thoroughfare of this quaint western town. The stage stopped in front of the mercantile, and I sighed in relief as the stage stumbled to a stop. A week of waiting threatened to make me daft. Waiting and wondering.

With each mile we traveled over the last few days, I worried. Would my husband find me beautiful despite my dark skin and eyes? Would he desire me? Would he be kind or cruel? I did not worry over his looks, for I knew a handsome face could hide an evil heart. My entire life, I had been treated as an outcast, the bastard child of a wanton woman's wicked pleasure. Tainted. I could withstand harsh judgment, but hoped for kindness. In the deepest, darkest place in my soul, I hoped for a man's love, but that was too grand a dream to ever speak aloud.

No. I worried most what my husband would think of my two sisters. They would be a surprise, something he had not expected. I hadn't been able to leave them behind with our uncle though. Because of my wanton ways, he was going to marry me to a man with six grown children. From what my uncle had told me, I was to be Mr. Partridge's third wife and as such, he wanted a lusty bed partner and not a simpering virgin. My uncle had told him of my unfortunate, licentious leanings, of my immoral background and the man had still been more than eager.

I, however, was repulsed. Mr. Partridge was fifty-two.

He was obese and had jowls. Food fell from his lips as he talked during a meal, landing unceremoniously on his shirt. To make the man even more odious and the arrangement completely ironic, he was very pious and committed to the church, which meant he expected me to be demure and meek when in public.

And a harlot in private.

I wondered if he expected me to eat his leftover dinner off his shirt as I undressed him for bed.

The only way to escape him was to flee Omaha. But if I left either Judith or Rebekah behind, surely our uncle would marry one of them off to him—or someone just like him—instead.

Accepting the offer made in that advertisement had been my last desperate attempt to save myself and my sisters. I understood, too well, that a man with two sons to raise didn't need additional mouths to feed, but we'd been desperate, so desperate, to get away.

Because of this, I would keep Judith and Rebekah a secret until after I was wed tomorrow. Only then could my new husband not send all three of us home. I'd gone mad, surely, but our uncle had finally pushed me too far. I took a deep breath, let it out. I could do this. I could do anything as long as I wasn't in Omaha. My husband might reject my sisters, but if I married, they could remain in Hayes as respectable women with the hopes of finding employment, or even husbands of their own.

If my new husband refused to help us? Well, the little money I had saved would keep us reputable for a few months. Hopefully, that would be long enough to see them properly wed. After that, I didn't much care what happened to me. I would survive, as I always had. As long as I was away from the pious Mr. Partridge.

In a rush to be free of the cramped quarters, we stepped down and landed in the middle of a group of men who were busy loading sacks of flour, tins of food and other supplies into the back of a wagon. They paused and looked our way, each and every man tipping his hat in our direction.

The group was large, at least ten men. Judith and Rebekah froze in place at the sight of them all, for they were quite large and very formidable. They exuded an aura of… power. It appeared that they were traveling, just passing through town to purchase supplies. I tried to imagine all of them housed under one roof at a hotel or boardinghouse, but rejected the idea. There was something wild and untamed about these men. Fearless and bold, like I imagined a great grizzly bear would be, ambling through the forest. I suspected men such as these slept beneath the stars with loaded guns at their sides.

"There isn't much to this town, Lizzie." Rebekah picked up her cream-colored skirts and looked around with a frown, clearly not as intrigued by the men as I. The top half of her dress was cut of a dark, velvet brown that brought out the gold streaks in her hair.

"I told you two the town was small." I tried to keep my voice low as I studied the men's laden saddlebags and filled wagon. While we were at our final destination, these men seemed to have a long way to go.

Pity. One or two of them might have made fine husbands for my sisters.

"It's nothing like Omaha, that's the truth." Judith stood

next to her sister, her blue traveling dress stained around the hem, but the dress' color a vibrant match for the cornflower blue of her eyes. "I hope your Jenkins is worth it, Lizzie. I'm going to miss having tea at Mrs. Dodd's house. Do they even have a hotel?"

My sisters didn't know of my uncle's arrangement with Mr. Partridge. They'd only fret or offer themselves up in my stead. As I wanted none of us yoked with that man, here we stood.

"Of course." I had asked the stage driver three towns back. If not, I'd planned on leaving my sisters at the last stop, in a reputable hotel, until I was a married woman and could safely retrieve them. Having them in Hayes was better. I wanted them close. Safe.

"Hotel's just up the street, ladies." All the air was sucked from my lungs at the deep, silky voice that slid over my skin like a caress. I recognized the accent from a trip to New York. If I wasn't mistaken, he was British, and these men were a long, long way from home.

"Thank you." I smiled because I couldn't help myself as I studied the two men standing side by side, one with a sack of flour over his shoulder. The other, the man who had spoken, was busy winding up a length of rope in large, rough-looking hands. My attention was drawn to the smooth glide of the rope under his hardened knuckles and I imagined the rough drag of those strong hands over my sensitive skin. Both men were both dark-haired and tall with closely trimmed black beards creating an air of danger and mystery that made me shiver. They were handsome. Intense, almost brooding... and looking directly at me.

They looked me over—me, not my sisters—taking in every inch of my body, their gazes tracking every curve of the simple yellow fabric that covered my ample breasts and wide hips. I flushed, remembering how bedraggled and filthy I must look. I'd never been at the receiving end of such blatant stares. How long had they been on the trail? Too long, if they found me more appealing than either of my younger, fairer sisters.

Judith and Rebekah were beautiful with their pale hair and creamy skin. They were just over a year apart in age and were often mistaken for twins, except Judith's eyes were a pale blue and Rebekah's green as spring grass. I looked more like a complete stranger than their sister. While they took after our mother in size and coloring, I had the darker looks of my father, who I had been told was my mother's biggest mistake.

As golden as my sisters' hair was, mine was black and straight. My skin was warmly brown year round and tanned at the lightest kiss of the sun. My sisters were petite and classically beautiful while I looked like a giantess standing a half head taller, my shoulders wider, my breasts and hips full. If my sisters were lovely reeds swaying in the river's wind, I was the large, sturdy cottonwood lining its banks. We were as different as night and day. We shared a last name because our father had adopted me when he married my mother. We were the Lewis sisters, but I was the bastard. The black sheep.

The daughter of a tainted woman, inheritor of both her wicked tongue and wanton blood. Neither made me acceptable company in our small, God-fearing community. If our father hadn't been the minister, I'm sure I would have been stoned to death by age fourteen.

Still, the two men near the wagon looked at me and I saw desire darken their eyes. They looked at me now the way the two men I'd seen the night before looked at the naked beauty between them, with want. Lust. Need. The memories of what I'd witnessed were what made today's stage journey tolerable. I couldn't think of much else. What maiden could? Instead of being horrified, as I should, I was envious. I tried to clear the image from my mind, but it was too late. All I could think about was being shared by them, just as naked, wanton and wild as the woman I'd seen.

My heart leapt into my throat as they continued to eye me and I fought for breath. The man tossed the sack into the back of a wagon with an ease that showcased his strength and the breadth of his shoulders. The other continued to coil the length of rope, watching me, slow and patient as a cat stalking a mouse. Every long inch of them screamed rugged cowboy and I made fists of my hands so I would not reach out to touch what did not now, and never would, belong to me.

I lowered my eyes and turned my attention to the tattered tips of my shoes, ashamed. I was ogling men who were not my intended husband. My wicked blood was going to ruin this chance for us if I didn't get myself back under control. What would Mr. Jenkins say if he knew the naughty thoughts filling my head to overflowing? And still…

Hope flared in my chest. If this was the caliber of man to be had in the Montana Territory, I couldn't wait to meet my new husband. Perhaps he, too, would be ruggedly handsome. Strong. Perhaps he would make my heart skip a beat and my nipples peak beneath my dress like these two did.

Perhaps one of these men was Mr. Jenkins himself?

Surely not. It couldn't be possible, could it? At our last stop, I'd sent a message ahead to Mr. Jenkins telling him we would arrive in three days' time. I felt a small twinge of guilt for lying to my betrothed, as it had been only two since I sent the message. Mr. Jenkins was not expecting us today, and I was eager to hurry along, to have Judith and Rebekah safely settled in our hotel room, hidden from sight, until after the wedding was over. With only a few stagecoach runs to Hayes, worry took root in my chest. What if he were as anxious as I? What if he came a day early to look for me?

Taking a deep breath, I relaxed my tense shoulders. No. Fate would not be so cruel to me, not after she had taken me this far. I could believe nothing else.

That meant that none of the handsome men before us were Mr. Jenkins. As confirmation of that, none of the men, while they enjoyed looking at the three of us, stepped forward to claim me. I had been sure to send Mr. Jenkins a recent photograph, so he had my likeness, but none of these men had two small sons in tow either. Disappointment was bitter on my tongue as I pasted a smile onto my lips and lifted my chin high. Mr. Jenkins would be wonderful. He simply must be. I was sure of it.

The driver dropped our bags at our feet with the disinterest of a man who had ten more miles to ride before bed. I afforded him a small smile of thanks, then picked up the bag that held my meager belongings. The summer day was warm, but a slight breeze reminded me that fall was on the way. I was thankful for my thin coat, but knew we would need my husband to purchase heavier winter things for us before the ice and snow took hold.

"Let's find our hotel," I said to my sisters, offering them a small smile.

The cruelty of our uncle may have pushed me to agree to marry a man and be mother to his children through a newspaper advertisement as a means of escape, but I wanted to at least freshen myself and have a good night's sleep before I faced my future. Tomorrow, I would be strong again. Tomorrow, I would meet my new family for the first time and allow myself to fall in love with my new sons. Tonight, I would close my eyes, put my feet up and enjoy my last day of freedom.

I urged my sisters to walk ahead of me onto the board-walk, passing *them* as we carried our bags to the hotel. The two men I'd noticed earlier turned their heads and continued to look at me as I went by, tipping their hats. I told myself not to look. I swear I did. But it was like they possessed a secret power over my body and my eyes refused to listen to my head. I glanced at the closest man and a shiver raced down my spine at the intense interest I saw there. His friend, a few steps farther, drew my attention directly thereafter. His gaze was dark and thoughtful, but he looked at me as if he knew me, as if he knew my secrets and could see straight into my soul.

I held my breath as I passed in a vain attempt to avoid the spicy scent of their bodies. They smelled so much better than I'd expected. Sweat and dust and the odor of horses clung to the air, yet these men smelled of wild pine trees and earth.

"Miss," the second man said, his voice rough and dark and deep.

Up close, I could see that the first had green eyes; the other's were dark as coffee. I should have been wary or even fearful of their unswerving attention. Instead, I felt... hot all over. Lightheaded, as if I would faint. My heart was practically beating out of my chest and my nipples tightened beneath my corset. I pulled my thin wool coat closed around me, thankful it would hide that embarrassing fact, and forced my feet to carry me forward.

As I turned away from them and headed toward the hotel at the end of the block, I could feel them watching me, their gazes like fire tracing a mark on my back. Once in the hotel room, my sisters took over the bed to rest. I stripped out of my dusty clothes. Standing before the mirror, I saw my scrubbed complexion. No matter how much soap I used, how much I scrubbed, I would always feel dirty. Years and years of living with my uncle had reinforced that notion.

Tears of exhaustion filled my eyes as I washed my body. My nipples were hard and when I cleaned myself between my thighs I felt a hot ache there. I knew the throbbing fullness wasn't caused by thinking of the man I was to marry, but of two rough and handsome cowboys, and a tear slid down my cheek.

CHAPTER 4

ogan

"WE'VE BEEN all over the world and we find *her* in the Montana Territory," I muttered, shaking my head. The black-haired beauty had met my gaze, met my fire with her own. I knew what desire looked like on a woman, and suddenly all I could think about was seeing her hot and naked under me, her body glistening with sweat and my name falling from her lips as I made her beg for release. "Damn it."

I wasn't cursing the woman; I was cursing the rock-hard cock taking up too much damn room in the front of my pants. Less than a minute and a complete stranger made my cock so hard and full it ached.

I dropped a bucket of nails onto the back of the wagon

31

with a loud rattle. A few spilled out and I grabbed them, tossed them back into the tin. There was no denying it; the dark-haired beauty that had alighted from the stage was the woman for me. And I'd clearly heard one of the lovelies say the name Jenkins. These women were about to fall into a terrible trap. After what that little shit, Samuel Jenkins, and his sons had said the night before, it was our duty to protect the women. I just didn't know *which* woman was his bride. Nor did I care. Not one of them was going to be touched by Jenkins or his filthy sons, not while I lived.

"Which one do you think is the future Mrs. Jenkins?" I asked Ford, who was standing still as a statue watching the women as they walked toward the hotel. He turned to glance at me as he reached down to the front of his pants and adjusted his own problem. I laughed. "Please tell me that hard cock is for the dark-haired beauty."

"I don't know which one is for Jenkins, but I know the one that's for us."

"Please say the dark-haired one, because I have no doubt that she's ours," I grumbled. This was a serious moment and I had no interest in jests.

"Hell, yes, the dark-haired one. Kane warned me that when we saw her, it would be like this, but bloody hell." He rubbed his chest. "She's ours. No question about it." He shifted his cock again. "If you want to marry her and fuck her senseless, then yes. I agree."

"Good. Now that I've seen her, now that I've looked into her eyes, I want her. She's walking away and it's actually painful. I want her in our bed by nightfall." Ford's green eyes slanted with determination as he lifted his gaze to follow the women as they entered the front door of the hotel. "We have to marry her today. That's the only way we can make sure Jenkins doesn't touch her. Hell, I don't want him touching any of them."

"Agreed."

The other men in our group circled around, none willing to allow Mr. Jenkins and his sons to defile such beauty as we saw alight from the stage. "Which one is Jenkins' bride?" Evan spoke up, but our entire group was intense and focused. We had a mission here, and couldn't leave town until we all made sure those women would be safe.

I frowned. The Jenkins men hadn't described the woman last night, only what they were going to do to her. We hadn't even been able to get a glimpse of the photograph. The idea of those bastards touching any of those women made me want to cut off their cocks and stuff them down their throats so they choked, but it was the eldest woman Ford and I had just agreed to claim.

"Doesn't matter. The dark one is ours," Ford said and I added my agreement. Somehow, I preferred the one who didn't have milk-white skin. The other two were pale and fair-haired, but the eldest—she was clearly a few years older—had hair as dark as midnight and her skin had been kissed golden by the sun. Her lips were full and soft and her eyes held definite interest as she looked at us. When she'd glanced at me, then at Ford, and stilled, my cock had turned rock hard. I saw the truth in her eyes. She'd felt it, too, an instant connection. Want. Right then and there, her fate had intertwined with ours.

The other men nodded at Ford, understanding our

interest. "How you know she's yours, like that." Garrett snapped his fingers. "It's beyond my understanding."

"You just haven't seen your woman yet," Ford told him.

"And you can't have ours." I felt the need to emphasize our claim. I, too, would have asked the same question if it hadn't felt as if I'd been kicked by a mule when her dark eyes met mine. I wanted her hot and wet beneath me. I wanted to taste her skin and her pussy. I wanted to explore every inch of her body and discover all her secrets.

"The younger two—the blondes—are surely sisters," Evan offered.

The other men nodded. That the younger girls were related was impossible to miss, for they looked similar enough to be twins.

"It's unusual that three women just happen to come to this tiny town in the middle of nowhere. Today." Evan stroked his beard. "It's not often we see three lovely ladies out here at all. Hell, it's been months."

"Since Fargo, at least," Thompson added, grumbling. "And those green eyes. Damn. They were full of fire and ice." He reached down to adjust his own cock and Garrett laughed.

"Brown dress? Golden hair?" Garrett asked.

Thompson looked at Garrett and a nod of understanding passed between them. I lifted my fingers and snapped them in front of Garrett's face. "Just like that," I said.

We were not used to going hundreds of miles without the sight of a lovely lady or two. Back home in England, a simple stroll down the street would provide dozens of lovely, high-bred women. Problem was, none of them would accept the lifestyle we'd all embraced during our time in Mohamir. Two men sharing a wet, willing woman between them was, to us, the ultimate pleasure. The uptight mothers and fathers of London would not be able to accept our ways.

In addition to our heathen sexual practices, we were nothing but retired soldiers, not dukes or earls. Except for my friend Ford, we were all simple working men, not titled nobles. We had no hope of living life our way back home, so we came out here, to the Wild West, to the Montana Territory where we could live the way we wanted at Bridgewater.

"Perhaps there's more than one man who sent for a mail-order bride?" Evan's question pulled me from my thoughts as he glanced at Daniel. Those two had agreed to share a bride, just as Ford and I had. "Daniel, did you get a look at the one with the blue eyes?"

I hadn't noticed the eye color of the two blond women for I'd only been looking at *her*.

Daniel nodded with a lust-filled grin. "Absolutely."

"Are we agreed then?" Evan asked for confirmation of his choice, just as I'd asked Ford. He wanted the blue-eyed woman to be their bride.

"Agreed." Daniel nodded his head in the direction of the hotel, then laughed. "Hell, you'd think we just negotiated for a new horse, but shit, I want her. I want her and no one is going to get in my way."

Evan slapped him on the shoulder, for this was how it seemed with all of us. We just… knew.

"How are we going to accomplish this rescue? We

don't know anyone in this damn town. For all we know, the sheriff or local judge might be Jenkins' cousin."

"I don't care which one is Jenkins' intended bride," Ford said. He placed the coiled rope on top of the sacks of flour. "That marriage is *not* going to happen."

"There's only one hotel, so we know where they've gone," I said, looking in that direction.

"We'll take shifts watching the hotel so they don't suspect," Evan offered, stroking his beard. No doubt he and Daniel were eager to get another glimpse of the blue-eyed lady.

"We'll watch the Jenkins men," Garrett offered and his friend Thompson nodded agreement. "They were drunk, stumbling their way to the stables last night. We'll head over there and keep them away from the hotel." They put on their hats and left the group. The others surrounded the wagon and I nodded to each of our brothers-in-arms. They knew the stakes. Three women meant three brides. Three beautiful women to take to Bridgewater.

I nodded my thanks. "Why don't you boys take the wagon and meet us at Bridgewater Ranch? We'll be a couple of days behind you."

"Done." I didn't know which of the men had spoken, nor did it matter. Six men were headed to Bridgewater, six staying in town to rescue three lovely women. The Jenkins boys were drunken idiots. They were no match for us.

Ford stepped up onto the boardwalk as the wagon pulled away. I expected him to head for the hotel, but he turned in the opposite direction. I bit my tongue and balled my hands into fists. My inclination would be to tear her hotel room door down, swoop our future bride over my shoulder, and ride out of town. But that's why Ford had been our spy and scout while I always hungered for the rage of taking down my enemies on the front lines. I tended to be a charging bull, but I wasn't stupid. Ford would have a plan. The bastard always had a plan.

I fell in step beside him. "Where are we going?"

Ford's grin was full of the devil and I grinned back. "To find the town preacher."

"What if she won't agree?"

"She will." Ford slapped me on the shoulder, just as Evan had Daniel. "Trust me."

I shook my head. "If she's got a sense of honor, she'll insist on meeting Jenkins first. Sounded like she gave the man her word."

"I know. And she's going to keep it."

"What the hell are you talking about?"

We'd reached the front doors of the small town chapel and Ford grinned as he pushed open the door. "Just play along. She'll be ours by nightfall."

Hell if I was going to argue with that. I followed him inside and squinted for a moment as my eyes adjusted to the dimly lit interior of the tiny chapel. A small, nervous man walked forward between a dozen rows of hard wooden pews. He was close to sixty, bald, wearing dark robes, spectacles and a serious expression.

"Welcome to our chapel, gentleman. What can I do for you?"

Ford took off his hat, bowed his head and took on a

very contrite look. When he opened his mouth, I was shocked to hear a nearly perfect American accent. "Well, preacher, I was hoping you could marry me and my miss. We got a little carried away last night and I need to make an honest woman out of her."

The preacher's cheeks flushed a dark pink at Ford's plain speaking, but he cleared his throat and straightened his shoulders. "Well, has the lady agreed?"

"Of course. I never woulda touched her, sir. I swear. I didn't mean to, but I just got lost for a minute. She smelled so nice and she was so soft, and her kisses made me kind dizzy, and... well..." Ford shuffled his feet and hunched his shoulders in shame. I hid a gut shot of laughter behind a coughing fit as he continued. "Well, I love her, see. Now I need to make it right." Ford's smile was pure happiness and I wondered in awe at his acting skills. This was the reason he'd been the spy. Me? I preferred to shoot first and ask questions after.

"Very well. The Lord would approve of your dedication to your future wife." The pastor frowned up at Ford, just to make sure my friend understood that he was a sinner. "But he would have preferred you had waited until the wedding night."

Ford spun his hat in his hands and looked at the preacher's feet. "I know. I'm sorry, but I want to make it right. I want to marry her right away. Today, right away, if it pleases the Lord. My Lizzie, she's a good girl, sir. I want her to be right with the Lord."

The preacher sighed and crossed his arms. "All right. Bring your bride to me, Mister... what's your name?"

"Jenkins, sir. Ford Jenkins."

I blinked, slowly, so I wouldn't give away Ford's lie.

The name got the preacher's attention and he raised his eyebrow. "You related to Samuel and his boys?"

Ford looked dumbfounded, his eyes wide and innocent. "No, sir. I don't know no Samuel. My daddy's name was George. I'm from St. Louis. This here," Ford pointed at me with his hat, "he's my cousin, Logan Green. He sailed over from England to start a ranch with me. He's gonna be my witness, sir."

The preacher tilted his head, but obviously decided he was in full control. "All right. The church will require ten dollars to register the license due to the expediency and… delicate nature of the ceremony."

I was about to choke the man for extortion but Ford just nodded his head and agreed like a schoolboy obeying the teacher. "Yes, sir. I'll bring ten dollars to the ceremony." Ford paused and looked down at the preacher with pleading eyes. "You won't say nothing to embarrass my lady, will you? I don't want that. I don't want her to know I told you nothing. She's a good girl, sir. On my word, she is."

"Very well." The preacher pulled a watch from some hidden internal pocket of his robes. "I'll be wanting my lunch first. I'll meet you here at two o'clock."

Ford held out his hand and shook the man's with exaggerated enthusiasm. "Thank you, preacher. We'll be here."

I tipped my hat and followed Ford out of the tiny chapel. A quick glance at my own timepiece made me frown. We had three hours to convince our bride to marry Ford and accept me as well.

Three hours.

Short of seducing the woman, I wasn't sure how the hell we were going to pull this off.

lizabeth

THE SOFT KNOCK on the door drew my attention and I hurried to answer it before the noise disturbed my sisters who napped on the bed. We had all bathed and done our best to refresh ourselves, but unlike my sisters, I had been unable to rest. Being here, in this town, hours away from marrying my intended made my stomach twist in knots. Worse, fantasies about the two cowboys I'd seen earlier danced behind my eyelids every single time I tried to rest.

I opened the door slowly, peeking around the edge. Dark green eyes met mine, and a smile so warm I forgot to breathe until the lack of air made me dizzy.

"Miss Lizzie?" The cowboy I'd seen earlier, lusted after really, took his hat from his head and placed it over his heart. His dark hair had a crease in it and I ached to brush it away with my fingers. "You are Elizabeth from Omaha, aren't you?"

Unsure what to do, I opened the door a bit and stepped out into the hall, gently closing the door behind me. "Yes." I tilted my head as the second man came into view, his dark eyes intensely focused on me as I tried to speak past the sudden lump in my throat.

The green-eyed man held out his hand, palm up and I stared at it like an idiot. "I wasn't expecting you until tomorrow, Lizzie, but I'm honored to meet you at last. I'm Samuel Ford Jenkins, but my friends call me Ford."

Oh, my Lord. My knees threatened to buckle right out from under me and I backed up against the door, holding onto the handle at the small of my back for support. "Oh!" I couldn't breathe. This couldn't be real. It was too incredible to be real.

But it was. His smile changed from friendly to that of a man interested in more than a passing hello and he studied me. I knew my face was flushed, my breasts heaving quickly beneath my dress as I struggled to get enough air into my lungs. He was stealing every bit of it from this small hall.

"I'm sorry I didn't approach you properly when the stage arrived, but I was expecting you tomorrow, and well, you just surprised me, is all."

I sighed in relief when he finally broke the lock he had on my gaze and turned to the dark-haired man behind him. "This is Logan. He's my closest friend and is going to help me look after you."

Logan stepped forward and held out his hand as well. Ford stepped back so they stood side by side, a wall of well-muscled male. His hand fell to his side and I realized I'd just been incredibly rude to my future husband.

Straightening my shoulders, I stood and placed my hand in Logan's large palm. "How do you do?"

His hand closed over mine and I stilled as his thumb massaged the back of my hand, sending heat to pool low in my belly. "It's a pleasure, Lizzie."

A deep, low voice sent chills up my spine. My sisters were the only ones to call me Lizzie, but from these men, while it sounded odd, I liked it.

Ford cleared his throat and I forced myself to look away from the dark pools of Logan's eyes. I shouldn't even be looking at Logan; I should only have eyes for my intended. Pulling my hand from Logan's gentle grip, I turned and looked up, way up, into Ford's deep green eyes and said the first thing that came to mind. "I didn't know your name was Ford. Why didn't you tell me?"

He shrugged, and his grin was charming. "Well, I don't know. I was afraid you wouldn't come. Samuel is a respectable name, and Ford is… well, it's an oddity around here." As he spoke the words, he stepped back and lowered his head to look at the hat he now twisted in his hands. His strange behavior made my nerves start to twitter in alarm and I nearly jumped when he spoke again.

"There's something else you should know, Lizzie. I lied to you. I don't feel right about it, now that I see you, but I did. What's done is done." He raised his chin and met my gaze, his eyes full of contrition. "I don't have boys, not yet. I thought…" He cleared his throat. "Well, I thought you'd like me better if I could offer you more of a family. You went on so much about yours, well, I just…" He reached out and touched my cheek with his fingertips in a caress so tender I almost pressed my face to his hand. "I'm sorry I lied. I don't have children. Not yet. I want pretty little girls with ribbons in their hair, and sons, strong, strapping boys. But I want them with you, if you'll still have me?"

And there it was, my future and my opportunity. As quickly as my anger flared, it died, for I'd been keeping secrets, too.

He dropped his hand to his side and I cleared my throat. It was now or never. He'd seen my sisters when we got off the coach. I might as well tell him the truth now, when I had the upper hand and he owed me a favor. "I lied as well, Mr. Jenkins."

"Ford, sweetheart. Call me Ford."

"Ford." His endearment warmed me like a hot fire on a cold winter morning. "I lied as well. I didn't come alone. I couldn't leave my sisters behind. I was hoping…" It was my turn to look contrite and I bit my lip as my nerves threatened to spill out of me and make my voice wobble. My future hung in the balance, my sisters' safety and happiness, too. All would be decided in the next few moments. "My sisters, the women who were with me on the stage, well, I brought them with me, hoping it would be all right with you. I hoped you would help me look after them for a bit, until they get settled with husbands of their own."

Ford and Logan both smiled wide at my words. I would have been confused, had I a moment to gather my

44

thoughts, but Ford's words flooded me with relief and I was none too eager to question it.

"Of course. They're your family. Which means they're my family now."

The weight of a thousand worlds lifted from my shoulders, a weight I'd carried for so long I didn't realize how great the burden until it was gone. "Thank you!" I couldn't contain myself; I leaped forward into his arms, smiling and filled with unbelievable relief and joy.

His shocked stance cooled my enthusiasm and I worried that I'd overstepped my bounds, but when I tried to pull back, strong arms closed around me and pressed me tightly to his chest. I didn't even think to struggle. This man was mine now, or would be soon.

Fate was being kind indeed.

He held me for a long minute and his scent filled my lungs as the long, lean strength of him heated my blood. I wanted to melt into him. His hand traced the long line of my spine through my gown and his deep voice rumbled in my ear where it was pressed to his chest. "I've got the preacher waiting to marry us, if you're ready."

"Yes." I nodded, tears welling in my eyes. This man would be my new home. His touch was gentle, even for a man of his formidable size, his eyes sharp with intelligence, and his soul kind, for he'd not batted an eye at agreeing to care for my sisters.

If I were being honest with myself, I had begun to fall in love with him a little right there in the hallway of the hotel.

Logan shifted behind us and I turned my head to meet

his gaze. "You'd best gather your things, Miss Lizzie, and your sisters', too," he told me. "We've got business waiting at home, Ford. We need to get out of town before nightfall."

My heart sank a bit at his words, for I'd dreamed of a wedding night spent in a hotel room such as this, with a warm, soft bed beneath me as my husband made me his. My mind brought forth images of the loaded wagon I'd seen earlier and I frowned. "How far away is your home? You never told me that."

Ford squeezed my shoulder and stepped back to look down at me. "Not far, sweetheart. Not far."

I would have asked more questions, but he didn't give me the chance. I opened my mouth to speak, but he covered my lips with a hot kiss, his firm lips coaxing a response from me that I was only too eager to give.

The wanton devil inside me took control and I lifted my arms to wrap around his neck. I buried my fingers in his hair, eager to feel the soft strands glide over my skin as I pressed my breasts to his hard body.

His tongue invaded my mouth, my soft gasp of surprise immediately followed by a moan I could not stop from escaping as he plundered, stroking in and out like I'd witnessed the night before, like a hard cock taking my mouth. As Ford explored my mouth, his hot hands landed at the small of my back, but I wanted them lower, cupping my ass, pulling me hard and rough against his cock.

I wanted so much more than this kiss. And this man, at last, would give it to me. *My husband.*

"We have to go, Ford." Logan cleared his throat and Ford seemed to come back to his senses. Pity.

Ford ended our kiss, but I couldn't make my body stop

shaking. He stared down into my eyes and I felt like I was drowning. "You are a wanton little witch, aren't you?"

His words acted like a bucket of ice-cold water and I bit my lip, pulling out of his arms completely, my spine stiff as I fought off tears. I looked down at the floor. When was I going to learn to control myself?

"I'm sorry. I'll wake my sisters and gather our things." I turned to go back into my hotel room. I'd messed up already. I'd lost control, shown him that I was unclean.

Tainted blood. Unclean. An unwanted bastard.

My uncle's harsh words circled in my mind like vultures picking at my soul, but Ford's hand came to rest on the back of my head and he turned me around to face him with a commanding touch that kicked my bruised heart back into a fast race.

"Don't ever apologize to me, Lizzie. Not for enjoying my touch." He stepped close and placed my hand over his heart where I could feel it racing to keep pace with my own. "Do you feel that? I want you so badly I can't breathe, sweetheart."

Doubt clouded my vision for a moment, but then his rough thumb traced my bottom lip and just that quickly, I was his again.

"Get your things, sweetheart. The preacher's waiting and I want to make you mine as soon as possible."

God help me, I wanted that, too. I nodded and went to wake my sisters.

CHAPTER 6

As I escorted Lizzie down the boardwalk to the church, I was acutely aware of Logan keeping pace behind us with her two sisters. He was holding on by a thread, and that kiss in the hallway hadn't helped matters.

I felt badly about it, for taunting my friend for all of a few seconds, but I'd needed to know she could handle us both. I needed to know whether or not she had any fire.

The truth was, she burned so hot I'd nearly lost control. I'd damn sure forgotten where I was, lost in the plush feel of her lips, the surprised innocence about it. About her. I'd forgotten everything, including the danger we would all face if we didn't get Lizzie and her sisters out of town as quickly as possible.

As we passed the stables, I looked up to find Garrett

49

and Thompson watching us with eyes like a hawk's. Garrett's gaze inspected their chosen bride, as Thompson nodded to me and pointed at the saloon.

So, the Jenkins boys were recovered and already drinking once again. That would make our escape easier.

Evan and Daniel stepped forward from the front of the mercantile as we passed and I introduced Lizzie and her sisters. While the men tipped their hats for all three, they only had eyes for the sister named Judith. Ford handed off the women's bags before we walked on to the church.

Unable to resist touching her, I reached for her hand, pleased when she allowed my touch and did not attempt to pull away. I'd seen the darkness and doubt cloud her gaze when I'd called her wanton. I did not know what vile things had been spoken to her in the past, but once she was mine, she would not be allowed to think so poorly of herself or her passionate nature. As long as that heat was for me and Logan, there was nothing shameful. It was a gift we intended to take great pleasure in exploring.

I held open the door of the small chapel and allowed the women to walk in first. Logan nodded as he took the door from me and we both confirmed that Thompson and Garrett had moved their positions to guard us from across the street in case the real Samuel Jenkins got wind of Lizzie's and her sisters' presence in town. This wasn't Mohamir and death wasn't a possibility, but we weren't risking anything with Lizzie's fate in danger.

"Ah, Mr. Jenkins. Welcome back." The preacher stepped forward and I shook his hand. When he did not step away, I remembered the ten dollars I'd promised and slid the money, discreetly, into his hand.

The ceremony was quick, just the way I wanted it. When the preacher asked Lizzie if she'd take 'Mr. Jenkins' to be her husband, I quickly corrected him and asked them both simply to call me Ford.

As the entire thing was a bit out of the preacher's usual, he simply shrugged and Lizzie agreed to take me, Ford, as her husband, to love, honor and obey.

My cock grew hard as a rock as I watched her full lips mouth those three words and I had to force my mind to function as I took my own vows.

I kissed my new wife as I had in the hallway of the hotel, exploring her mouth as I intended to explore her pussy, deep and hard and surrounded by her wet heat.

Behind me, Logan prowled like a caged tiger, eager to mark her as well. But as fierce a soldier as Logan was, he knew when to wait. We had to get Lizzie away from this town before we could tell her the truth and introduce her to our ways. Soon enough she would understand that she didn't belong to only me, but to Logan as well. Soon we would take her body between us and share her as we intended. Soon she would beg us to bring her pleasure over and over again.

"You're mine now, Lizzie."

"Yes." Her eyes darkened at the heat in my voice and I wanted to rip her dress from her body and take her here, rut into her on the floor of this damn church like an animal.

I thanked the preacher who shook his head. "I understand now, the need for expediency."

"What?" Lizzie turned to him, a confused expression on her face.

I scowled a warning at the preacher as I signed the church ledger. I made sure to sign my real name, and instructed Logan, as witness, to do the same.

Unless my new wife inspected my signature, she'd have no idea I wasn't Mr. Jenkins until it was too late to annul the marriage. I would take her innocence within hours and nowhere near Hayes. I wanted to ensure there was no way Samuel Jenkins had a chance to steal what was now mine. Short of killing me and Logan, Lizzie would be safely out of his clutches forever.

And if he decided to kill me?

Well, the drunken sot was welcome to try.

"Come along, sweetheart. I'd like to get you home as quickly as possible."

My near growl made her cheeks turn an adorable shade of pink and I pretended not to notice Logan adjusting himself as he followed us outside to a waiting group of men.

Lizzie's sisters halted dead in their tracks at the four large men waiting for them outside the church. Daniel, who had been carrying their bags, handed them off, Judith's bag to Evan and Rebekah's bag to Thompson.

I lifted my hand and made the introductions. "Ladies, I'd like you to meet my friends. You've met Evan and Daniel. The other two are Garrett and Thompson. Lizzie, they will escort your sisters to the ranch and make sure they're safe."

The ranch just so happened to be Bridgewater, but for the moment, the vagueness of the response was important. I needed the sisters to go off with the men knowing they'd be protected and arrive safely before us. The fact that none of us had been there before was the portion Logan and I would tell her about later. I had no doubt the men would inform Judith and Rebekah once they were away from town.

Judith's blue eyes flared wide and she turned to Lizzie with a fearful expression on her face. Lizzie, in turn, looked up into my face with a question in her lovely brown eyes. "I'm not sure about this, Ford. We are in a strange place, with new people. Why can't they go with us?"

I leaned down to whisper in her ear, sure she wouldn't want the others to hear. "I plan on making you mine tonight. I assumed you wouldn't want an audience to hear your cries of pleasure."

Her eyes widened and I watched as her cheeks turned pink. Grinning, I happily watched the rapid rise and fall of her chest as she digested my words. She pasted a bright smile on her face and turned to her sisters. "It's all right. Go with them. I trust my new husband to see you are well taken care of."

Evan stepped forward and looked down into Judith's shocked features. He bowed his head and held out his hand to the petite woman. "You have my word of honor, Judith, nothing will harm you while you are with us."

Judith looked at up him for a moment, leaned around him to inspect Daniel, who nodded. "On my honor, you will be safe and protected, Judith."

She turned back to Lizzie with a sigh. "All right. I suppose it is your wedding night."

Lizzie stepped back as if seeking my strength and I was only too happy to provide. I positioned myself at her back, placing my hand around her curvy waist. "Rebekah. You'll be escorted by Garrett and Thompson."

Garrett lifted Rebekah's bag and held out his hand to her. "You will be protected as well, love. I, too, give you my word."

I noticed her hand shaking as she placed it in Garrett's much larger one and allowed him to lead her farther up the boardwalk, with a silent and brooding Thompson falling into step behind them.

Evan led a tearful Judith toward their horses and she waved, a watery smile pasted on her face as Lizzie leaned into me. "When will I see them again?" she asked.

"Two or three days, depending on the weather." I leaned down and kissed her temple. "Trust me. They'll be well taken care of. Safe. I promise you."

She nodded and didn't fight me as I led her toward our waiting horses. Logan carried her bag and I was grateful she didn't question his presence. Soon, she would know the truth of our ways, would be spread like a goddess between us. I could only hope she didn't hate us both when she learned the truth.

* * *

LOGAN

I ALLOWED Ford to take the lead with our bride, kissing her, touching her, making her feel safe since she believed *he* was her husband. I didn't really have a choice in the matter, not if we wanted to get our wife out of town without violence. We couldn't afford questions, not now, when she still believed she'd kept her word to one Samuel Jenkins. The bloody sod.

That didn't mean I had to like watching him get to feel all that soft skin, to breathe in her scent, to feel how silky her hair was, to feel her lips against his own. The bastard had what was also mine. If my cock were making the decisions, she'd be beneath me and no longer a virgin, but my brain was still working. Barely.

We rode for several hours, Lizzie draped across Ford's lap like a queen. I was in the lead, not wishing to see what I couldn't yet have. I took us on a circuitous route to get to the ranch, for I knew if we rode too quickly, we would meet up with the rest of our party with the wagon.

I didn't want to see them, not tonight. Tonight, we needed our bride between us, naked and wet. Tonight, we would seduce her into accepting both of us and we didn't need a damn audience. We needed privacy.

Two nights ago, the group had camped at a small creek nestled amongst the trees. The spot was well protected on three sides by canyon walls. While we weren't in Mohamir, at war or even in any kind of danger, our instincts would not allow us to sleep unprotected. I'd lain on my back, counting the stars, thick as a blanket in the sky, and imagined a new life of work and boredom on the ranch. A ranch! In England, there was no such bloody thing.

I missed the call of battle, the thrill of it, the rush of feelings it brought about. It was the only way I could release the aggression that seemed to build like a storm in my blood. Now that storm was focused entirely on one woman and a nearly desperate need to make her scream and writhe with pleasure. My new outlet for this energy would be with Lizzie. *In* Lizzie. She would obey me, she would ride my cock like a wild thing, and she would bear us children. I'd never wanted anything so badly in my life.

One day and my life, our lives, had changed completely. Life on a ranch didn't seem so bloody awful anymore, not with the prospect of a willing bride between us. We were going to a place that accepted my need—with Ford—to claim Lizzie. We were going to a place to join other men who we trusted with our lives. We were going to a place where all the evil we saw in Mohamir didn't exist. We were going... home.

Lizzie's soft voice drifted on the wind and my cock stiffened at her whispered words. "Why is Logan riding with us? Why did he not go with the others?"

I pretended not to hear as Ford answered her. "He's my brother-in-arms. We served many years together, fought together, nearly died together. I trust him with my life, and with yours. I share everything with him, sweetheart. He is yours now, as well. He will cherish you as I do and will protect you with his life."

"Oh." The simple sound made me smile as I led the way into a spot I decided was perfect to camp for the night. She still didn't understand, but she would. "I guess that's nice, to have such a close friend. Like a brother."

"Yes, but he is more than a brother to me."

Ford didn't say more, for he knew, as I did, that it wasn't the right moment. I didn't want to her to learn the full truth yet, not until I was ready to fight her shock, her fear, and help Ford seduce her to our ways.

The flat grassy area was beside a slow-moving creek. A deep section with still water called to me and I longed to wash the sweat and dust away, eager to be clean for our bride. I stopped my horse and quickly took care of the gelding as Ford did the same with his own animal. Lizzie wandered the small area, sneaking into a grove of cotton-wood trees to relieve herself as Ford and I both pretended not to notice.

Boots off, I waited until I knew she would return. A skittish virgin was like a mare, needing time to assess the stallion to determine him worthy. While I'd been witness to her passion when Ford had kissed her, it didn't hurt for her to begin to accustom herself to both of her men. Naked. As I caught a glimpse of her coming through the trees, I turned and pulled my shirt off over my head and dropped my pants to the ground.

Her gasp was my reward and I walked forward until I was hip deep in the ice-cold water. It did nothing to diminish my ardor, for my cock jutted up toward my navel, ready for her. I lowered myself, washing quickly. Ford stripped, too and strode into the water, scooping water up and using a cloth to scrub his body clean.

I rose from the water, grinning as I saw our passionate young bride standing stock still and staring. Her mouth was open and her eyes were squarely on my cock. I walked to my horse, drying off with a blanket as Ford left the water behind and closed the distance to our bride.

We had discussed how this would happen many times. We'd walked through a hundred different scenarios, discussing the best way to seduce a woman, what it would be like, how we'd take her. Claim her. Make her ours. We didn't need to talk, not now. We both knew exactly what we wanted and it was Lizzie. No other woman would do.

I heard Ford begin our seduction, asking the first question we needed an answer to. "Are you virgin, Lizzie? Have you ever lain with a man?"

She stumbled backward a pace, then held her ground. Clearly, she was not used to having a naked man, dripping with water, ask her about her maidenhead. I was pleased she didn't run away screaming, but knew having me stand directly beside Ford would be too much for her. Blanket around me, I wandered to the horses and hid myself somewhat from view, giving our bride the illusion of privacy with Ford.

"Aren't you going to get dressed?" she squeaked.

Ford shook his head. "No. Please answer my question."

"Your… question?"

"Have you been with a man before?"

I held my breath awaiting her answer. It didn't matter if she had, for she was ours nonetheless, but knowing we would be the first—and only—men to fuck her was potent.

"No. I mean, yes." She shook her head with a nervous laugh and tried to look everywhere but at Ford. Her chin even went up so she'd have to look at his face and not his bare body. "I mean, I've never…"

Ford stepped forward and pulled her into his arms—she, fully dressed, Ford, as naked the day he was born. Her words faltered and I stepped out to watch once more as she closed her eyes, standing stiff in his embrace.

"Have you found release, Lizzie? Have you touched

yourself? Have you cried out alone in the night, wishing for a man's touch?"

She shook her head in earnest now, her face red with embarrassment. Shame. "I can't. It's wrong. I can't…"

"I'm your husband. There's nothing wrong about my hands on you."

"But Logan—"

"Logan thinks you're beautiful, too. I like knowing he's watching as I take off your dress." Her chest heaved as Ford began undoing the buttons at her neck. She didn't fight him, but stood still as a frightened bird caught in a trap. Her eyelids fell closed.

"But—"

"Shh," he crooned, silencing the last of her resistance. "Shh. Such a good girl." Ford didn't speak again until she stood naked before him. My cock roared to life as I took in the generous fall of her breasts, the dark hair between her thighs, and the ripe curves of her waist and hips. I wanted to touch. I wanted to taste. I wanted to explore every single inch of her. My balls ached to fill her.

Ford kissed her as I stalked closer, waiting for the perfect moment, for Ford's cue to join them.

He must have been good with his tongue, for she swayed and pressed her naked body to his without restraint. Her soft cries were music to my ears and I stepped up to them, just out of arms' reach of our new wife.

Ford held her face between his hands and kissed her closed eyelids. "Do you trust me, wife?"

"I—" she sighed. "Yes." There was no hesitation in her

answer and my cock jumped as if she'd stroked it with her tongue.

"Keep your eyes closed." Ford scooped her into his arms and walked to where I'd laid my blanket over a patch of soft grass. I knelt on the edge and he settled with her in his lap, his kiss ensuring she didn't notice my presence until he had her exactly where he wanted her. Leaning back against a saddlebag, he settled her so her back was against his chest. Ford hooked his ankles around hers, spreading her legs wider and wider. I shifted then so I knelt between her parted thighs, her glistening pink pussy on perfect display. I couldn't wait to taste her.

"Are your eyes closed?" Ford asked, although I could see they were.

"Yes." Her voice was barely there, a hasty thread of sound.

"Good girl," Ford added. "If you move without permission, lie to me or disobey my commands, you will get a spanking on your bare bottom. Do you understand?"

She scrunched up her face in confusion. "You'll… you'll spank me?"

"Mmm," he murmured against her ear. "I am beginning to think you would rather enjoy my firm hand on your bare arse." He pinched her nipples as he spoke, his lips tracing the elegant lines of her neck. "It's time to explore your pussy, wife. Are you ready?"

She shuddered in his arms but took nearly a minute to answer. I began to worry she would deny us, but when Ford's hands wandered lower, toward her wet pussy, she whimpered.

"Yes, Ford. Yes."

"Good. Keep your eyes closed, wife." His hands stroked and caressed her thighs as I fisted my own cock to try to relieve some of the ache. She moaned and twisted, trying to force his hands to her pussy, but he was stoking the fire a purpose, getting her ready for me, for my hands. For my mouth.

I glanced at Ford and while we were not mind readers, I knew exactly what he was thinking. She was a vixen, a woman filled with heat and passion. She would not be a frigid bride; instead, a wild wanton who would meet our needs. Just as we would meet every single one of hers.

He had been given the gift of touching her first, but I would make her scream. It had only been a few short hours since we'd seen her, but in truth, I'd waited my entire life for just this moment.

Ford took hold of the back of her knees and pulled them up toward her chest, exposing her pussy and tight virgin rosette to me. It was almost impossible to stifle the groan at the delectable sight. I wanted both. Now.

"But—"

"Keep your knees high, wife," he cut in. "Do so and we will give you pleasure you can't imagine." She whimpered as Ford stroked her pussy at last, his fingers tracing the delicate folds, moving several times to stroke her clit. I could see her arousal glistening there, watched as it trickled from her. She was not immune, she was… perfect.

Ford had deliberately said 'we,' but she was beyond hearing until Ford spoke again.

"I'm going to slide two fingers into your pussy, hard

and deep, just like you want it." He did just that and her hips bucked up off the ground. "Do you like that, wife?"

She moaned her assent and I moved forward, ready to take her with my mouth. She was almost ready. Ford repeatedly used the word 'wife' to assure her that this was all right, that her lust, her desire for a man's touch was perfect and natural. Right. So right. We would not be denied, but neither would she.

I met Ford's gaze as he gently slid his hand from her pussy and rested it on the blanket. With a quick nod, I settled between her spread thighs. Inserting my own two fingers into her wet heat, the hot glide nearly made me groan. Her inner walls clenched down on my digits and I almost came then and there. I wanted to bury my cock in her pussy, pound into her until she begged me to stop, to let her come.

She bucked against my hand, her head thrashing back and forth against Ford's chest, unaware that it was now me who touched her, me who explored her hot core with my fingers. Me, who would make her come.

I fingered her clit as Ford encouraged her. "Do you want to come, wife?"

"Yes."

"Do you want me to fuck you now, fill you with my hard cock and make you mine forever?"

"God, yes." She wrapped her hands around her knees and pulled them up, higher and tighter, wider, exposing her pussy to me like a pagan offering to a hungry god. Her nipples were tight little pink tips, begging to be suckled. Later. Now I would taste her.

I couldn't wait for Ford's slow seduction a moment

longer. I lowered my tongue to her clit and latched on, sucking hard and deep as I fucked her with my fingers. She was sweet like honey on my tongue and I was ravenous. I wasn't exactly gentle, for I was too far gone to tend to her as a sweet virgin, but she did not behave as one. She reveled in having her eyes closed, at the feel of a man between her thighs. Her body relaxed against Ford's, giving over to the intensity of my tongue, the thorough coaxing of my fingers. I wanted to stretch her open, to prepare her for my cock, for she really was an innocent and I did not wish to hurt her. Our cocks were large and we would prepare her accordingly in both her pussy and her ass.

I heard her shocked cry, felt her pussy clench down on my fingers once again, and I knew she'd disobeyed. I glanced up to find her eyes firmly on me, round with shock.

Ford whispered in her ear, "It's all right, sweetheart. Logan is yours, too. Your husband. We share everything, love, and we will share you. You'll scream with pleasure that we both give you. Look at the way he sucks on your clit, love. Feel his fingers fucking you, making you come. Feel how much we want you, how beautiful you are. You are a goddess, Lizzie. We are yours. We will die to protect you. You are safe with us. Let us worship you. Let us make you scream."

Ford's hands cupped her breasts, pulling and tugging on her nipples as I devoured her pussy with my mouth and tongue. I didn't give her a chance to think, simply found the soft spongy spot inside her with my fingers and returned all my attention to her clit, suckling and licking as Ford continued to arouse her not just with his hands, but his words as well.

Relentless, I gave her no chance to start thinking. If she did, she'd think this was wicked, might ask us to stop. She'd think she was dirty for wanting two men, for getting wet for them. For coming for them. It wasn't dirty. It was perfect between us and I would prove it by making her come all over my mouth and fingers.

I pushed her, fingering her carefully, although with her obvious arousal now coating my hand, she took me easily. I felt her virgin barrier break and she stiffened once again. I gentled then, suckling her clit until she panted and moaned, until I felt the walls of her pussy clamp down on my fingers once more.

I sucked hard then, tonguing her clit until she screamed, her back arching off the ground and her thighs coming down to lock around my head like a vise.

But I had no interest in escape. I would die a happy man between the thighs of my wife.

Once her body stopped milking my fingers, when she relaxed against Ford, I kissed her inner thigh, then sat back on my heels.

Not giving her a moment of reprieve, Ford lifted her, moving her high on his chest until his cock was aligned with her pussy. Taking hold of her hips, I slowly lowered her down, then let go entirely when Ford thrust up, filling her completely for the first time. He was fucking her from behind as she settled against his chest, her hard clit exposed. As Ford began to fuck her in earnest, I leaned forward and claimed her little clit, making her ours forever.

CHAPTER 7

 *lizabeth*

FORD'S COCK pushed inside me, spreading me so wide I wanted to scream and push away, but just as I was ready to protest, he seated himself deep within and held still, the sting fading to a full, stretched sensation that made me long to squirm on his thick cock. I wanted to move, but I could not.

My legs were wrapped around Logan's head, his tongue licking my clit like I was made of the finest cream. Trapped between the two men, images from the previous evening rose to taunt me with their wicked ways and I closed my eyes once more, helpless to fight the heat rising to claim me. I wanted it. God, I wanted them with desperate need, with a pleasurable lust that I couldn't deny.

They weren't hurting me—they weren't gentle, but I did not want that—as they took me. This was *taking*. Just like the men I'd watched at the hotel fuck their woman. I never knew a woman could be fucked in such a position, but I was so full I couldn't believe my body had accepted Ford's huge cock.

Ford held himself still inside me as Logan's mouth worked me. With his fingers, he spread my pussy lips wide, allowing Ford's cock to slide just a bit deeper into my body, all the way in, striking my womb with a sharp note that made me moan and attempt to lower my legs, but the moment I lifted my legs from Logan's shoulders, Ford's hands wrapped around my thighs, holding me open and wide, unable to move away from either his huge cock or Logan's tongue.

Logan bent his dark head, sucked and licked, driving me mad. It was almost too much, the overwhelming feel of being surrounded by both of them, taken by both of them, touched, fucked, sucked. God, it was almost unbearable.

I tensed, trying to break Ford's hold on my legs, but Logan shook his head and bit my clit gently in reprimand as Ford tightened his grip. "Don't move, Lizzie. Your body is ours now. We will make you come, love. We'll make you scream with pleasure. Just let go."

There was nothing I could do but give in to their touch. Ford held me in place, impaled on his hard cock, knees spread wide as Logan worked me with his tongue. It was all so intense that my back arched and my body jerked in an effort to escape the force of the release I felt building.

"Come for us, Lizzie. Come now."

I couldn't give over on my own, but Ford's rumbled command somehow pushed me over the edge and I lost control, screaming as my body bucked and shattered on his cock.

As I settled back to earth, Logan's kisses on my clit gentled into a warm exploration and I lay languid and spent in Ford's arms, his cock still buried deep.

But it wasn't to last. Logan lifted his head and sat back on his heels in front of me. Before I knew what was happening, Ford lifted us both and repositioned me on my hands and knees, his hard length never leaving my body as he moved behind me. *Just as I'd watched the night before.*

Hard hands gripped my hips as Ford pulled out so that just the broad head of his cock nestled inside, then pushed deep once more. His guttural groan of pleasure came with another command. "Logan made you come, love. Now it's his turn. Take his cock in your mouth."

I lifted my head to see Logan's thick cock within reach. It jutted from his body, dark and angry colored. Fluid seeped from the tip and slid down the thick length. *Take his cock in my mouth?*

As I opened my mouth to protest, to question why a woman would do that, Logan's thick length touched my lips. Ford slammed deep once more, moving my entire body forward, and the thick tip of Logan's cock filled my mouth. I gasped at the surprise of it all, which made Logan groan.

"Good girl," Logan said. "Lick it. Yes, like that."

The soft head fascinated me and I ran my tongue along its round rim as Ford pulled out and drove deep yet again.

Logan's hands were buried in my hair and I felt his growl of approval as I licked and explored his length. While the woman the night before hadn't had a cock in her mouth, she'd had two men pleasuring her, just as she'd been pleasuring them. I was the dark-haired beauty between two men, taking one in my mouth as the other fucked me from behind.

Fantasy merged with reality and I took Logan's cock deeper, sucking hard and fast before releasing him over and over, mimicking the rhythm of the hard thrust and release of Ford's cock in and out of my pussy.

Ford's hand slid down my back and his thumb brushed over my back entrance. I stilled and moaned around Logan's cock.

"Fuck, Ford, do that again," Logan said, his voice rough like tumbled rocks.

"Play with her arse?" Ford replied. "You like it when I touch you there, don't you? She's squeezing my cock. I don't know how long I'm going to make it if she keeps doing that."

His thumb, slick with my arousal, pressed into me. I wasn't as stunned by his actions as I should have been, as I would have been if I hadn't seen the woman the night before. I knew what came next, but Logan's cock was in my mouth.

All of a sudden, my body gave way and Ford's thumb slipped inside. There was a slight burning to being stretched in such a way, but there were too many sensations at once for it to bother me. Ford began to move then, fucking me with his cock and slowly fucking me in my back entrance with his thumb.

Logan's fingers tugged on my hair, distracting me from Ford's ass play. I wanted to make Logan lose control. I wanted both men to be mindless with lust, just like the two men I'd seen that night. I wanted to be the goddess between them now. I was the one who made Logan tug harder. I was the one who made Ford thrust deeper, faster. *Me.*

Logan's cock jumped and bucked against the roof of my mouth and I swallowed down the salty taste of his release. Ford lost all sense of rhythm and fucked me hard, hitting the top of my womb with every thrust of his hips.

Desperate for breath, I released Logan's cock from my mouth and tried to force air into my hot lungs. My body spiraled once more, a release just out of reach.

Logan knelt on the blanket and reached down to lift my chin. I looked up into his dark eyes and saw something there I'd never seen before. I didn't know if it was love, or lust, or reverence, but the look made me whimper with longing.

As he lowered his lips to mine, he issued a command to Ford. "Touch her, Ford. She's riding the edge." His lips grazed mine, quick and light and too fast. "Aren't you, my Lizzie?"

I licked my lips and he took them in earnest, bowing my neck up and back as he took the kiss he wanted from me, a hot, wet duel of thrusting tongues and desperate need.

He kissed me, pulling on my nipples where they hung

down over the blanket as Ford obeyed Logan's order to reach around my hip and stroke my clit once more.

Back arched, completely exposed to Ford's fucking and Logan's kiss, I shattered into a million stars, my vision hazy. There was no air to breathe, no Elizabeth. I no longer belonged to myself.

I was theirs now. Forever. In the darkest, neediest place in my soul, I knew the truth and it terrified me. I was tainted. Corrupt. I did not deserve such pleasure and would surely burn in hell for accepting it. My weakness for these men would damn me and my sisters both.

As my body came down from the spiral of need, I began to cry.

FORD

My BRAIN WAS foggy from the most incredible orgasm of my life and yet instead of having my bride settle comfortably in my arms, she started crying. As soon as I slipped my spent cock from her tight sheath, she stood, albeit on shaky legs, and ran from us.

I glanced at Logan, who looked as stunned as I felt. She'd come three times. Satisfaction was not her problem. As I tried to understand her reaction, she wandered toward the horses, her back to us. Her hair had come unbound and it hung long down her back, like a black silk curtain.

I shouldn't notice her body when she was clearly in distress, but I couldn't help but glimpse the upturned swell of her breasts. They'd been a handful, heavy and lush. Her nipples were no longer tight peaks, but plump pink buds. Her body was all curves, dips and swells. She was… gorgeous. She was also terribly upset.

I stood and slowly walked toward her. "What's the matter, sweetheart? Did we hurt you?"

She shook her head, but with her hands over her face, I couldn't read her emotions. Her tears didn't stop. In fact, my concern only made it worse.

Logan took another blanket from his saddlebag and wrapped it carefully around her shoulders. Instead of saying anything to her, he scooped her up into his arms and carried her back to the spot where we'd just fucked her.

"Put me down!" she cried, pushing against Logan's chest. Her face was splotchy red and tears streaked her cheeks. All her fighting was futile, for Logan settled on the blanket with her on his lap, her head tucked beneath his chin.

"Shh, it's all right to cry. Just go ahead and have yourself a good cry and then we'll talk about it."

I'd never heard such a gentle tone from Logan before, but when it came to a crying woman—*our* crying woman —he'd be whatever she needed.

Slipping on my pants, I let Logan tend to her as I took care of the horses, removing their saddles. As I did so, I watched as he whispered to her, stroked her back, her soft hair as she cried. She kept at it long after I let the horses graze and joined them.

When her tears turned to sniffles, Logan used the

corner of the blanket to wipe her cheeks. "Now, tell your men what's wrong. Are you hurt?"

She shook her head and whispered, "No, I'm not hurt."

"Did we scare you?" I asked. We'd been fairly intense, but we'd done nothing but give her pleasure.

"No."

"Then tell us what it is." When she turned that dark gaze toward me, I saw only sadness.

"I... I have my mother's wicked blood in me."

Logan looked at me over Lizzie's head and frowned.

"Why is her blood wicked?" I wondered. "Lizzie?"

She sighed. "My mother loved a man who wasn't her husband. I was born from that union."

"You mean she was married and had an affair?"

Lizzie shook her head. "She fell in love with an Indian, and my grandparents refused the match. I'm proof of their union, of her going against their wishes. She was banished from the family, but before they could marry, he was killed. With nowhere to turn, she went back to her parents. They refused her. She went to live with my uncle, her brother. He... he was not happy, but he was a pious man and charitable to take a fallen sibling into his home."

Logan loosened his hold about her, allowing her to sit up. The blanket slid and one pale shoulder was exposed.

"He married her off to a man from church who would have her—and me. They had Judith and Rebekah. I was very little, but I don't remember much. I do remember her scent. Lemons and cinnamon. I remember her hair; it was as fair as the girls. She died when I was seven, run down by a stage beside her husband. I think it was from a broken heart."

I could see the sadness on her face, hear it in her voice. I could not share the depth of her mourning for a child to lose a parent, but I certainly knew of a loveless—and forced—marriage. I knew the result of it, the hurt, the devastation.

"My sisters and I were taken in by my uncle." She shuddered, turning her head to look at me, the bleakness gone from her eyes, replaced by anger. "Judith and Rebekah are perfect. Sweet, kind, meek. Just as young women should be. I am—not."

Logan stiffened, but continued to stroke her back through the blanket.

"You seem pretty perfect to me," I commented.

"I have the appearance of my father. A permanent reminder of my mother's sinful ways. I have her weak will, her tainted blood, her lustful body. She was a whore and now, so am I."

She tipped her chin down.

"A whore? You were a virgin until a few minutes ago and you gave yourself to us, your husbands."

"Yes, but there are *two of you*. And I *liked* it. I *liked* having both of you touch me. I *liked* what you did. It's not right. It's just not."

While I heard the frustration in her voice and tears filled her eyes again, I could only feel relief. "Liking what your husbands do to you is not shameful."

"I'm not supposed to have *two* husbands!" she shouted. Her voice carried on the slight breeze. The sun was just beginning to set, but the air was still warm as she continued to rant at us.

"I didn't reply to your advertisement or agree to be

73

your wife so I could be in a sinful relationship with two men. I am an honorable woman. I gave you my word. I trusted you to do right by me. God, I even brought my sisters with me. I've ruined their lives. This is not right. I'm not right." Her hands twisted in the blanket across her stomach in obvious distress. "My uncle was correct. I must have evil inside me. I've ruined everything."

Bloody hell. I flicked my gaze to Logan, who closed his eyes for a moment, then nodded. We had to tell her the truth. I didn't want to do it now when she was hurt and sad, but she deserved to know.

"No, you didn't. But you've done nothing wrong. You answered an advertisement and agreed to marry a sixty-year-old, filthy miner by the name of Samuel Jenkins. He sat at the poker table with his two grown sons, reeking of sweat and piss, bragging about how they were all going to share you between them. Fill you with three Jenkins cocks."

I raised my hand to her cheek and tried to soften the blow I'd just dealt. "I took one look at you, love, and knew I could not allow such an evil man to touch you. If your distress is anyone's fault, it's mine. I lied to the preacher, and I lied to you. I am not Samuel Jenkins."

She blinked. Once, then twice. "What?" She scrambled off Logan's lap as if she'd been scalded, tucking the blanket tightly about her. From the neck down, only one slim ankle was exposed.

We didn't move, but Logan grabbed his pants and put them on as I spoke.

"My name is Ford. That is the truth. My *full* name is

Crawford Michael Ellison, the seventh marquess of Barton."

Her mouth fell open. Narrowing her eyes, she stared at Logan. "Then who are you?"

"I'm Logan Smythe. Son of a merchant. A soldier. And your husband."

With one hand clenching the blanket she pointed between the two of us. "You planned this. You *tricked* me. Why? Why me? My sisters are beautiful, and, and pure. Not like me." She laughed then. "God, it's amazing. You stole the wrong woman, for you have married a half-breed bastard with tainted blood."

She knelt down and grabbed her dress, turned her back and dropped the blanket to don it. I could see my seed dripping down her thighs mingled with her virgin's blood.

"Where are you going?" I asked.

Once she had her arms through the sleeves, she spun around and spoke as her fingers moved up the buttons, hiding her curves as she went. She was too angry to realize she had not put on any undergarments.

"Going? Back to Hayes to find the *real* Mr. Jenkins. I don't believe you. He courted me. Wrote me letters. You've lied about everything else, why should I believe you about him?"

"That's it? You're going to go back to search for a vile, disgusting liar, just because he was *supposed* to be your husband?"

"Yes. I'm no longer virgin, but perhaps he'll forgive me." Squatting down, she tried to lift one of the saddles, but she only moved it a foot or two before she grunted and exhaled. The horse was grazing a short distance away, but there was no way she could toss it over the animal's back. She hadn't even put the blanket on first. "I have to do the right thing. Going back is the honorable thing to do."

I think I fell in love with her in that moment. She was riled, her cheeks flushed from her ire, her hair a wild tangle, long down her back. She was breathing hard and I couldn't help but watch the gentle sway and press of her breasts against the front of her dress. Knowing that she was sticky with my seed only added to the possessive heat flooding my chest. She was fierce and loyal and stubborn and passionate and… needy.

She needed a man who would see her passionate nature for what it was: a priceless gift given to a vibrant woman. The fact that she loved the way I'd fucked her, had come from both my cock and Logan's mouth meant our connection was powerful, not that she was tainted. She was perfect. She was mine. She was *ours*. We simply had to earn her loyalty. She would be the perfect wife, a powerful and fiercely protective mother to our children and a wild vixen in bed. We just had to make her fall in love with us.

lizabeth

I WAS MARRIED to the wrong man! A marquess? Whatever the heck did that mean? It didn't mean a darn thing to me. He was a liar and a thief. And he wasn't Mr. Jenkins. I was married to a man who lied to a preacher. I was married to a man who *shared* me with his friend. And I'd liked it.

No, worse, I'd loved it. I'd come all over his cock and wanted more.

My tears fell once again.

Hadn't I cried enough? I tugged at the saddle for a third time. It was too heavy. There wasn't a chance I could lift it onto the horse so I could ride back to town.

Very well. I'd walk. I stood and wiped my cheeks and headed back the direction we'd come.

"Where are you going?" Ford asked.

"Hayes."

"The sun is about to set. It's five miles away and you aren't wearing shoes."

"No water. No food," Logan added. "And there are snakes."

I stilled then, feeling the cool grass beneath my feet. It was lush and green here by the water's edge, but it would soon become tall and dry. I knew how far we'd come and I certainly couldn't make the return trip on foot. My fancy high-heeled boots weren't made for trudging across empty prairie, nor were my bare feet.

My legs collapsed and I dropped to the ground in a swirl of my long dress.

I heard the men's footsteps.

"Go away." I didn't look at them. I never wanted to see them again. Ever.

"You're my wife. I won't ever leave you." Ford's words should have been a balm, but were an irritant instead, reminding me I was stuck with him. For the rest of my life, unless I could get back to town and find Mr. Jenkins. Get the marriage annulled.

But they'd taken my maidenhead, consummated the vows. Was an annulment even possible? And if I went back to town, would Ford get into trouble? Had he broken the law? And why did I care? Why did I have this stupid weakness where he and Logan were concerned? I wanted to slap his face so hard I'd leave a welt for the lies he'd told. But I knew I would also long to crawl into his lap and kiss it better. Angry as I was, I still wanted to kiss them, feel the scrape of their beards on my lips and between my spread thighs, the rough edges of them both nudging my breasts and parting my knees.

God, what a mess. I was a mess. My confusion was like oil poured on a fire, making me even angrier.

"You achieved exactly what you wanted, sir. Or is it *my Lord*?" I crossed my arms over my chest and stared out over the knee-high grass that bent and swayed in the breeze. Far off, a prairie hawk cried out, circling high above the land, gliding with such peace and grace that, for a moment, I wished I were a bird, not a woman. Life would be so much simpler.

"It's Ford. I'm just Ford. And what exactly did I achieve?"

I knew he stood behind me, but he did not come closer, did not attempt to touch me.

"Fucking. You fucked me just as you wanted. Like I was a whore to be mounted." The hawk dove to the ground as I watched and my anger rode with it. I imagined the feel of a mouse's head crushed by hard talons, the wild joy of ripping the small, helpless animal to shreds with a sharp beak.

"Yes, I did. We both did. We fucked you hard, Lizzie. We made you beg and scream." He bent low over my shoulder, his lips inches from my ear, his hot breath a torment on my still sensitive skin. "And we're going to do it again."

I swear I saw red in that moment because I knew they could. The passion that drove me wild when they touched me was redirected into rage. I stood, spun about and lunged for him. Before I could hit him, he grabbed one wrist, then the other.

"How dare you!" I tried to kick him in the shins, but my bare foot didn't do much damage and I only hurt myself. Tears stung the back of my eyelids, but I refused to allow them to fall.

His green eyes were close but held no anger. While his hold was firm, it wasn't tight. I was the one out of control, but he held me still with a gentle touch and forced me to listen.

"If I wanted a quick fuck, I could have gone to the saloon and bedded an actual whore. I didn't have to get married. I wanted you and now you are mine. You belong to us and we won't give you up. Are you listening to me, wife?"

His words didn't make me any less angry, but they were getting under my skin, making me feel even more confused about what was going on here. Why me? Why had they done this? "I don't understand. Why? I was promised to another."

"I wanted you the first moment you stepped off that stage," Ford said.

"I did, too." Logan added from beside us. I hadn't heard his approach. I was so close to Ford that I couldn't see anything but my husband's face as he looked down at me, patience in his voice.

"We married you because we knew you were the one with whom we wanted to spend the rest of our lives. We would not dishonor you by stealing your virtue. And we could not allow you to marry Jenkins." He leaned down and placed a chaste kiss on my forehead as I struggled to hold on to my anger. "Your virginity was a precious gift you shared with us. Your husbands. Our connection is strong. The pleasure we found in each other, incredible. How is that not perfect and right?"

Was he purposely being daft? "You *stole* me from Mr. Jenkins. Perhaps *he* was the perfect man for me. Perhaps I would have had a connection with him. He is one man. One husband, as is right. And I gave him my word."

Ford lowered my hands to my sides, which pulled me in even closer to his hard chest. I had to tilt my chin up to look at him. His eyes roved over my face, then met my gaze.

"Do you know *why* we married you?"

"You just told me!" I shouted. "Lust at first sight. You simply had to have me. You're like a pirate, taking whatever you want."

Logan circled around, behind Ford, and stopped to stand beside us. "We understand you're upset, sweetheart, but you do not have to be insolent."

I bit my lip, but made it clear I was not happy by narrowing my gaze. His response was to laugh. How he could find humor in this situation was beyond me. Ah yes, Logan wasn't legally married to me and he'd had his cock sucked. *He* was the only one free to walk away from this… predicament. But he didn't move away; instead he moved in closer, until they both towered over me, making me feel small and helpless—and aroused. I stared at Logan's lips as he began to speak.

"Mr. Samuel Jenkins is approximately sixty years old. He is missing a front tooth right here." Logan pointed into his mouth. "He favors chewing tobacco and bathes about once a month."

I shook my head, unable to process more lies. "No, he just turned forty in January."

Ford shook his head. "His two sons are in their twenties and are *very* eager to make your acquaintance. They planned to share you between them once the old man was finished with you. They bragged about it last night at the saloon." While his fingers tightened on my wrists, it wasn't because he was trying to hurt me, but because of ire, and it wasn't directed at me.

This couldn't be true. It simply couldn't. "No. He wrote that his boys are small, still in primary school."

"Did he also tell you that the older boy, Tad, is nearing thirty, a half head taller than I, and eager to fill you with his seed?" Logan asked. "Or that his younger son, Harry, has only ever fucked whores, but he and his brother have a reputation for treating a woman so rough that the prostitutes in town refuse to service them?"

I thought back to the boring, if somewhat vague last letter I'd received. "Well, no. He said his two sons would need my—attention." I sucked in a breath and tried not to toss the contents of my stomach onto the hard ground. "Oh, my God."

Logan ran his big, strong hand up and down my back as if that would help soften this blow. Did I dare believe them?

Looking up into Ford's too serious gaze, I realized that I did. I believed every word. "Samuel Jenkins *was* planning to marry you, Lizzie. That was the truth. He was also planning on sharing you with his fully grown sons."

I tugged at Ford's hold and he released me, but I didn't go anywhere.

"What was it that he said?" Ford asked Logan. "Oh, yes. He said that any child would be a Jenkins, no matter whose seed took root."

I gasped, more than confident I understood exactly what that meant, especially now, with Ford's seed sliding down my inner thighs. How could this be true? Would a man be so cruel as to lie about everything and send for a woman—a woman who was desperate to escape her current life—only to dishonor and abuse her in such a way? It was abhorrent.

I glanced between Logan and Ford, one then the other, then back. They looked at me steadily, waiting. They weren't lying. I could tell that every word of it was the truth. Bile rose in my throat at how close I had been to living trapped in a new kind of hell. Perhaps remaining at home and marrying my uncle's choice, the stodgy and formal Mr. Partridge, would have been better. He stunk of tobacco and lamp oil, and had grown children, but I doubted he'd planned to *give* me to them to fuck.

"What about you?" I stuck my pointing finger in the center of Ford's broad chest. I was angry and hurting, and hating all men in general at the moment. "You married me and shared me with him."

"I did," Ford responded quickly. He wasn't denying it? "All of the men you met in Hayes are from the same military regiment. We were stationed in Mohamir. Have you heard of the country?"

I nodded, for I read every newspaper I could get my hands on, always had. Much to my uncle's discontent.

"Their custom is designed to protect and treasure their

83

women. Each woman deserves more than just one man to marry and care for her. To cherish her."

I felt the sincerity of his words and my hand drifted over my racing heart. The wild swing of emotions over the last couple of hours was taking its toll, and the abused organ actually ached as if I had a fist inside my chest squeezing the wounded heart of me.

Logan's rough voice took over the telling of their story. "Mohamir is a wild place, the country unsettled and remote. Their customs ensure the woman's safety and well-being. Should one husband die, his widow will not be alone or unprotected. Neither will her children." Logan's voice gentled on those words and I imagined him with a bouncing, laughing baby on his knee, and his strong, protective arms holding a wee babe to his chest, rocking a little one to sleep at night. "We spent many years fighting, watching our friends die. We faced death many times ourselves and we know, too well, how short life truly is. We adopted their custom, Lizzie, so any woman we claimed would be well protected, her safety and well being placed above our own. We have simply been waiting for the right woman to claim."

"You," Ford said.

Something they said had taken a moment to sink in and my new understanding startled me. "The others, Daniel and Evan, and the other men, *they* follow this custom as well?"

"Yes," Ford offered.

"My sisters are with them!" What were the men going to do to them? Seduce my sisters, as Ford and Logan had seduced me?

"Your sisters are safe. You heard the men. They will protect them with their lives," Logan insisted. "And they will not touch your sisters. They are not rapists, Lizzie. They won't touch an innocent, not without the vows of marriage and a woman's consent. They are honorable men. I give you my word."

My panic receded to simmering worry for my sisters as Logan's words settled in my heart. Perhaps my mind had been addled by the pleasure I experienced at his hands, but I believed him.

"We kept you from marrying Mr. Jenkins to protect you." Ford lifted my chin with his fingers, forced me to look at him. "But I wanted to fuck you, Lizzie. We wanted you hot and naked between us. We married you out of honor, but we lied solely because we could not risk that your own honor would have forced you to marry Mr. Jenkins. I have no doubt, given the fire I've seen the last few hours, that our suspicions were correct, and you would have confronted him about his intentions. Either way, we could not allow his evil to touch you. As your men—your husbands—your safety comes first, even if you aren't happy with our actions. We will do what's best for you."

"We would do it again, Lizzie," Logan added. "You belong to us now, and we will protect you with our lives."

I blinked back tears—damn them!—as I considered their words. "Was Jenkins really that bad?"

From the tightness in their jaws and the way Logan clenched his fists, I had my answer.

I wasn't content, was not ready to absolve them of what they'd done. But the rage, the shame that nearly choked me had weakened from a raging flood to a slow trickle. I'd think on their words, consider all they had said. Even if I went back to Hayes and confronted Mr. Jenkins, I was still married to Ford.

I was his for—oh, my God. I *wasn't* married to Ford. I was married, by proxy, to Mr. Jenkins. I had the paper in my bag to prove it. The man at the newspaper had signed it for me to take, ensuring that Mr. Jenkins could not return me.

"What is it, sweetheart? You've gone pale."

The men were too perceptive for their own good. These men had gone to great lengths to save me from marrying Mr. Jenkins and all their work was for nothing. They'd fucked me when I belonged to another. I tried not to laugh at the sick humor. I was truly tainted. I'd lain with them and I wasn't married to them. Yes, I'd shared my body with them when I believed Ford to be my husband. Ford and Logan had taken my innocence while believing I was Ford's legal wife. We had all been mistaken.

The truth was, I was Mrs. Samuel Jenkins. Legally, I had married the man before I ever set foot on that back-breaking, bone-rattling stagecoach.

What was I going to do? I couldn't go back to Mr. Jenkins. Not now, knowing what I did about him and his sons. I couldn't run away. The money I had wouldn't last long, and even if I could escape, if I left these men I might never see my sisters again. I was well and truly trapped, doomed no matter what choice I made. Just like that damn mouse in the hawk's killing grip.

God, what were Ford and Logan going to say when they discovered the truth?

A shiver sped up and down my spine and I closed my eyes against the cold chill racing over my skin.

First, I had to reunite with my sisters. After that, I'd figure out what to do about my marital status. My predicament was utterly absurd. Never had I heard tale of a woman who had not just one, but three men who could claim to be her husband. If my pious uncle thought me reckless and wanton before, he'd most likely die of apoplexy if he could see me now. One man's seed coating my thighs, another's down my throat, and a third man actually my legal husband.

Logan and Ford both watched me with concern and I shook my head, hiding my thoughts behind a heavy yawn. I had no idea what to do. I needed time.

"Nothing. I think I'm just tired," I replied, trying not to let my panic show. Based on what they said, I didn't want to be Mrs. Jenkins. But I wasn't sure I had much choice. I blinked against the grit in my eyes, leftover from the trail, and what felt like a thousand tears.

Neither man touched me as they walked with me back to the blanket. They tucked me beneath a second blanket and made sure I was comfortable. "Where are we going tomorrow?" I asked.

Ford stroked my hair out of my face as I closed my eyes. "Bridgewater. Tomorrow we go to Bridgewater and start our lives together."

Together, but with a tainted, already married woman.

CHAPTER 9

ord

I EXPECTED Lizzie to be subdued, to work through the truth of the situation and come to terms with her new life. I could only imagine how overwhelmed she felt, coming off the stage and then marrying within a matter of hours. Only later, she discovered she'd been tricked—even if it was in her best interest—into marrying someone else, only to find out that her new husband shared her body and claim with his closest friend.

I'd always assumed we'd court our bride slowly, give her time to adjust to the notion of two husbands, to fall in love with us and want to be with us as desperately as we wanted to be with her.

Circumstances ensured that was not the case. Bloody fucking hell. The only way to make this fiasco any worse

89

is if Jenkins came after us. I didn't expect that to happen, for I had signed my real name in the church's ledger. Jenkins would have no reason to link us to his bride, as the group I travelled with had only been in town for a couple of days to rest and purchase supplies. We were strangers, just passing through. No one knew us or where we were headed. Our final destination, Bridgewater Ranch, was not well known or nearby. And the three women had been separated from the group. Even if they tracked the wagon, they wouldn't find Lizzie or her sisters.

But then, according to Lizzie's confession in the hotel hallway, Jenkins wasn't expecting three women, just one. And that one special woman was now with us.

No, with both Hayes and Samuel Jenkins behind us, Logan and I just needed to be patient and let Lizzie accustom herself to it all. To us. I had to hope that having her meet the other Bridgewater brides would help.

Once Lizzie had fallen asleep, Logan and I agreed we'd push through to Bridgewater instead of spending a second night on the trail. The sooner we were settled, the better it would be for all of us.

We kept watch, splitting the long hours, one of us holding Lizzie safely in our arms as the other stood guard. Lizzie woke with the dawn and was eager to be reunited with her sisters. We rode hard all day and arrived at Bridgewater's stable just in time for the evening meal.

On our approach, two men came out of the large building. We knew the ranch was well established; money was not a concern with these men. Kane was a nobleman, the same as I. Funds weren't unlimited, but damn close.

Out here in the territory, so was our freedom to live as we saw fit.

I hadn't seen Whitmore Kane since we were in Mohamir, three years ago. It had been an unpleasant time, for our commander had killed a Mohamiran family and framed Kane's best friend, Ian, for the crime. He, along with Kane and several others, fled Mohamir directly for America. The remainder of the regiment, myself and Logan included, finished our service but chose not to re-enlist. Despite the fact that Ian had vanished, he was found guilty and sentenced to hang for his alleged crimes. Logan and I knew the truth and chose not just to leave our dishonest commander, but also the government that failed to fully investigate his crimes. Kane's invitation to join him in the Montana Territory was simply too tempting to refuse.

Kane grinned at our arrival and hugged us fiercely. "Reinforcements have arrived. I was worried that we'd lose the advantage with all the Americans homesteading around here. Good to have some fine English blood around."

Kane was tall and dark, very similar in appearance to me, but I was somewhat rough around the edges, he more refined. Despite being born a marquess, I gave the appearance of a rake or the untamed pirate Lizzie had named me.

"It is good to finally be here." I turned as a second man approached. He was large and dark-haired, but I did not know him.

I swung my leg down and dismounted my horse to stand in front of Logan as he helped Lizzie off his horse to stand on wobbly legs. I took her hand and tried to pull her to me so I could introduce our bride, but she tugged back hard as Kane greeted his friend.

Thinking perhaps Lizzie was feeling a bit shy, I turned to coax her forward. It was not shyness I saw in her eyes, but shock, followed by a dark flush that would have been intriguing had she reacted that way to anything but a virile, available male. I tugged on her hand once more, but she would not move, simply stood in place, her feet firmly planted as she stared at Kane's friend with wide eyes.

What the hell?

I glanced at Logan, who shrugged. He had no idea how to explain Lizzie's odd reaction either.

Giving up for the moment, I turned back as Kane spoke. "Ford and Logan, this is Xander."

The large man grinned and tipped his hat in our direction. "Pleased to meet you both."

Lizzie gasped at the sound of his deep voice and I turned to inspect her. Her breathing was rapid and her cheeks a pink I had only seen once before, when we made love to her. Had we kept her too long in the sun? Had hours of hard riding made her delirious? Was she taking ill? "Lizzie, are you all right?"

"Yes. Yes. I'm sorry." She stepped forward when I gently pulled her toward me and Logan took up a protective stance on her opposite side. She was between us, exactly where she should be.

With Lizzie sorted, I turned back to Xander. "Nice to meet you as well. That's not a British accent."

Kane chuckled. "While he's American through and

through, he's a Bridgewater man. He and Tyler, who you'll meet at the house, are married to Emily."

We shook hands and the man seemed affable enough. He, too, was dark and had a beard, but he was much stockier, much more solid than either Logan or I. Perhaps his size is what frightened our bride. I had no other explanation for her behavior.

"May we introduce our new bride, Elizabeth," Logan said. When he saw the way she was staring at Xander, he lifted his hand to the nape of her neck with a possessiveness I, too, felt. The confusion I saw in his gaze most likely matched my own.

Giving her hand a quick squeeze, I broke her from her reverie. She greeted both men, smiling at Kane but blushing hotly as she looked at Xander.

"Ma'am." Xander's eyebrows rose in curiosity, but he must have been raised right, for he didn't comment on her obvious upset. Nor did he step forward, keeping his distance.

"How long have you been married?" Kane asked.

I couldn't help but grin. "Yesterday." I still felt like the luckiest man alive, and wasn't above gloating.

Kane laughed. "Well then, a celebration—and a bed— are certainly in order."

Xander offered to tend to our horses as Kane walked with us to his house.

"We eat meals as a group on most occasions. My house —the one I share with Ian and Emma—has a large kitchen and dining room for it. We're growing quickly, we now have baby Ellie. There are a few others who have children. Christopher and Abby are toddling about as well. With your arrival, and the addition of your other men—wait, where are the others? We were expecting a dozen."

"Six are on their way with the wagon of supplies," I explained.

The house before us was large white clapboard with an expansive porch. It was set back from the other buildings by a fair distance. In fact, all of the houses and work buildings were far apart. While Bridgewater was turning into a community, it would seem everyone still wanted their privacy. I approved. I had no desire to share Lizzie's cries of pleasure with the other men on the ranch. That sweet sound was for her husbands' ears alone.

"I expect them to arrive tomorrow. Four more are traveling with Lizzie's two younger sisters."

Kane nodded, taking the news in stride and not asking unwelcome questions. We would tell him everything, later. All too easily we fell into our old custom. War and hardships were not to be discussed in front of the women. Kane smiled pleasantly at our bride and she seemed to relax once we'd left Xander behind. "Are you from these parts, Lizzie?"

She smiled and chatted with Kane as he showed us his home. She was much more in control than she had been at the stables and it was clear she had issue with Xander. Had they met before? How was that even possible? Had he somehow threatened her? Did he remind her of someone she feared from her past? As I tried to make sense of it, I realized how little Logan and I knew about our wife, and how badly I wanted to remedy the lack.

"No, from Omaha."

"You are a lucky woman then, meeting these two.

There aren't many men who I would trust with my life, but your husbands rank high on that list. You've got good men, Elizabeth."

His words were profound, and the trust and respect mutual.

Holding open the front door, he let us enter first. With my hand at the small of Lizzie's waist, we met everyone. *Everyone.* Faces that were familiar. Ian. Brody. Mason. Simon. Rhys. Connor. Dash. It was exhilarating to be with them all again, this time safe from Evers and the law. We also met Cross, Tyler, Andrew and Robert. Quinn and Porter, two of the foremen, were with Xander in the stables, but would join us when the meal was ready. Then there were the brides. Emma, Laurel, Olivia, Emily, Rebecca and Allison. The children brought the brightest smiles from our bride, and I knew we'd made the right choice, bringing her here. There were three children, all quite young, but they were bright, happy beings and I watched Lizzie closely, noticed the softening of her eyes and the bright hope that took root in her.

So, our lovely lady wanted children. I'd be happy to give her a dozen.

With this large of a group and knowing how the men must tend to their brides, surely the ranch would be overrun with young ones soon.

Perhaps even one or two of our own.

Logan took Lizzie by the arm and escorted her around the room, introducing her to everyone. She smiled and nodded, shaking hands when manners dictated she should, but I saw the lines of strain form beside her eyes, noticed when her smile changed from natural to brittle. She was being completely overwhelmed.

I didn't blame her. From what she shared, her childhood was less than warm and this brood would be quite an adjustment. When her sisters arrived, perhaps that would help, but their arrival would also bring ten more men.

Dinner was a loud affair; there was enough catching up and telling of old war stories to go late into the night. While Lizzie ate her share of roast and potatoes, she remained quiet. That was expected, as she knew no one but me and Logan, but she continued to eye Xander, along with Tyler and their wife Emily, with a mix of nervousness and obvious interest.

Leaning down, I whispered in her ear, "You seem scared by Xander. Has he done something to upset you?"

A piece of bread was halfway to her lips and she paused, then put it in her mouth. I saw it for what it was, stalling. The way her cheeks turned red, I knew that she'd had *some* kind of interaction with him. Whether I needed to punch the man in the face was yet to be determined.

She shook her head.

Ford glanced at me over Lizzie's head. "Xander's done something."

"No, he hasn't." She took a sip of water, then turned to me. "Truly."

"Xander," Logan said. The man turned his head and raised his eyebrows to indicate he was listening. "You don't live here at Bridgewater?"

"No," he replied. "We have a ranch past Helena. Kane bought some of our cattle a few years ago, then Tyler's sister, Olivia, married those three besotted fools." He pointed to Rhys and Simon, who I knew from my days in Mohamir, and a third man who had been introduced as Cross. Three husbands? Interesting. I didn't have much time to ponder because Xander continued, "Now Tyler and I come back to Bridgewater a couple of times a year to make sure they're treating his baby sister right."

At the other end of the table, Rhys and Simon shouted insults at Xander for insulting them. Cross bent Olivia over backward and kissed her senseless, right there in front of everyone. It was all in good fun and I watched Lizzie's eyes widen in alarm, then surprise as Olivia kissed him back, passionately, and the rest of the women seated around the table merely smiled with that look women get when the men they love are acting like idiots.

"You're just visiting then?" Logan pressed for more information as Lizzie stiffened in her chair, taking three times longer than it should have for her to chew that piece of bread.

Tyler put his hand across the back of Emily's chair. "We bought a bull past Lewistown and wanted to make a trip of it. We arrived yesterday."

"We just missed you then," I added. "We were in Hayes just yesterday morning."

Xander offered a smile, but it was partially hidden by his dark beard. "We followed the stage line. Safer that way. Didn't linger in Hayes though. Spent the night at the town before. Nothing little town. Never bother to remember what it's called."

"Drummond," Tyler offered.

Out of the corner of my eye, I saw Lizzie's cheeks turn

pink and she stared at her hands, which were tightly fisted in her lap.

Nothing about Xander made me think he'd done anything untoward to Lizzie. So, what was wrong with our bride? Did she lust after Xander? Did she wish she'd married him instead? The thought made me angry, and I vowed to get her naked and remind her exactly who she belonged to at the earliest opportunity.

Logan seemed to be oblivious. Either that, or he was having fun pushing our bride as far as he could, looking for clues. "Lizzie was on the stage from the east that day. I'm surprised you didn't see her or her two sisters."

Emily tilted her head and looked at Lizzie. "I would have remembered seeing you, you are so pretty."

Lizzie lifted her head swiftly, as if Emily's comments shocked her. "Thank you."

The other women at the table added to the conversation then, voicing their jealousy for Lizzie's darker complexion. "No freckles!" Anne commented with a smile. "That is completely unfair."

"I love your freckles, wife. They provide the perfect map for kissing you all over." One of Anne's husbands, Robert, leaned across his plate to kiss her. Olivia's men had started it, but an air of sensuality had quickly settled over the room and the looks between the married groups in the room grew longer and more direct.

Lizzie blushed and murmured her thanks as the ladies around the table ignored their husbands' groping hands and attention as they continued to discuss her rare and exotic beauty. I agreed wholeheartedly, but her confused expression confirmed what I had already begun to suspect. No one had told Lizzie she was beautiful before. She wasn't used to hearing the words, and didn't believe them.

I decided then and there it would be my personal mission in life to change that. Our wife was the most beautiful woman I'd ever seen, and I would dedicate my life to making sure she believed me when I told her so.

The conversation veered toward the fall harvest, yet I had not had my questions answered. Later, I would ask Lizzie and she would tell us the truth, even if we had to spank it out of her.

 lizabeth

LOGAN AND FORD both watched me with too keen an interest through the rest of dinner. I'd handled myself poorly, I knew. But the first sight of Xander walking out of the barn, and all I could think about was the sight of his massive chest and strong legs, his flexing hips as he knelt behind Emily, his hand in her hair and his cock deep in her ass while her other husband, Tyler, fucked her pussy.

The sound of Xander's deep voice when he had spoken outside the stables had hit me unexpectedly and I was instantly flung back into my fantasies on that balcony. I remembered the deep sound of his voice commanding me —no, commanding his wife—to come.

And poor Emily. She was a truly beautiful woman. She'd been kind and welcoming at dinner, a genuine person with whom I knew I could become friends. Shame flooded me as I remembered what I'd believed that night. I'd mistaken her for a prostitute in that hotel suite, not their wife!

And sweet, gentle Olivia? I'd thought two husbands scandalous, but seeing the way Olivia's three men stroked her hair and kept her close, always touching her, watching her, and making sure she felt surrounded, loved and happy? After growing up with a cold stepfather, a disapproving uncle and a town full of people who referred to me simply as the bastard? I saw Olivia's happy glow, the attention she received, the acceptance. I choked on the admission, but I knew enough to know that the churning in my stomach was caused by an acute case of envy. I wasn't only envious of the way her men treated her, but of the contentment and happiness that made Olivia's skin practically glow. She was in love. She was loved. And she *knew* it. She did not doubt her men, or their feelings for her. She had not one husband who worshipped her, who found her beautiful, interesting and worthy, but three! She did not question their devotion or attention, simply accepted it as her due.

I was still shocked that Logan and Ford would want me at all. Inside, where the darkest pieces of my heart had long ago been ruined, I was still in pieces. I was broken and I wasn't sure I would ever be able to love and be loved the way Olivia did.

I walked silently between my husbands as Kane showed us to one of the new houses built on the property. It was small, only a main room—with a large fireplace, kitchen area and a dining table—a bedroom and a washroom. This, it seemed, would be our house until we were ready to build one of our own. Logan had been adamant that I help choose the location for our new home before the men could start building.

My own home. Children. A house full of family and friends and no one to bat an eye at the strangeness of one woman with two husbands. Sitting at that table, watching the women settled comfortably between their men, I'd felt something shift inside me as well. Hope. Though the new emotion was fragile, like a new butterfly's wings, it was growing stronger every moment I spent with my men.

For the first time in my life, I felt welcomed and respected. Seated between Logan and Ford, I'd not been without one of their hands on me during dinner, the connection so simple, but a powerful reminder that I would never be alone again. They made sure my plate was full, listened when I spoke, and surrounded me with such warmth and affection that I found myself laughing and teasing as I had not since before my mother died.

They made me feel safe. Protected. Free to be myself.

They made me feel important and beautiful.

In two days, they'd shown me more caring and respect than I had received these past years from my own flesh and blood. They did not disgrace or shame me for enjoying their touch. No. They demanded it of me.

Why did loving more than one man have to be wrong? Who declared it so? Surely my uncle did not have that power.

"All right, sweetheart, tell us about Xander."

I went to stand on the far side of the dining table, my hands placed on the back of the chair. "I don't know what you mean," I replied, not meeting their gazes as my cheeks heated, giving me away. Damn it! If only I had not been so aroused that night. If only I had not been so brazen and touched myself as I watched them. I could not admit that now. Not here.

Never.

Xander had done nothing wrong; he'd been with his wife, fucking her without any knowledge of being watched. *I* was the one at fault. It was just ridiculously hard to sit across from him—from all three of them— remembering how they'd fucked her, how they'd taken her back entrance with as much eagerness as her pussy, how she'd squirmed and begged, sobbed and gasped, demanding more.

"Lizzie," Ford warned. "It's our job to protect you. We can't do that if you don't talk to us. You need to tell us what's bothering you. Xander has done something to upset you and we need to know what it is so we can take care of it."

They were starting to get annoyed. "Truly. He's done nothing."

Logan watched me silently, his gaze missing nothing. When I refused to answer, he crossed his arms over his chest. "You can tell us now, or we can spank your arse a bright pink and you can tell us after."

I took a step back. "What? You'd spank me?"

I thought of Emily and how she'd enjoyed the way Xander had spanked her.

"You have to the count of three to tell us the truth." Logan came around the table, ducked his head and the next thing I knew, I was tossed over his shoulder like a sack of grain. "Starting right now."

"Logan, put me down!"

He carried me into the bedroom and dropped me onto the bed. I bounced once and tried to scramble as the men each took one of my ankles—now exposed by my dress, which had tangled and risen to mid-calf—and easily flipped me over onto my belly. As soon as my feet touched the floor, a hand went to the center of my back and held me down.

The hand was gentle, but Ford's voice was stern. "No secrets, sweetheart."

I tried to push up onto my elbows so I could look over my shoulder at them, but I could not move as Ford knelt beside me on the bed, one hand pressed between my shoulder blades, the other pressed to the small of my back where he held my dress up.

"What are you doing?" My head was turned to the side, my cheek pressed to the mattress. I knew what was coming. Logan said he was going to spank me like a three-year-old, but I hadn't truly believed him.

"You've been keeping secrets, Lizzie. Lying to us." Logan's rough hands massaged my ass cheeks through my drawers and I felt my pussy grow wet. Seconds later, he ripped the thin material from my body and threw it to the floor. Fresh air hit my bare bottom seconds before Logan's first, soft strike.

If that was a spanking, I didn't mind it. In fact, I wanted more. Ford's dominant hold combined with the sensation of offering myself to Logan, just as Emily had when Xander was behind her, made me nearly swoon.

"God, Ford. That swat made her drip with cream." Logan swatted me again as I bit my lip and closed my eyes against Ford's knowing gaze on my flushed cheeks. "She's so wet I could fuck her right now, take her hard and fast."

I moaned at his words and Ford's hand clenched into a fist high on my back and his voice was deeper than it had been before. "Don't fuck her yet."

I opened my eyes to find Ford watching me.

"Before she gets fucked, she has to tell us all her secrets."

Logan swatted me again and I squirmed in an effort to tempt him to touch me. I needed him inside me. His cock. His fingers. His tongue. I wasn't choosy. I wanted him to fuck me and pull my hair, just like Xander had done to Emily. I wanted to climb up Ford's body and ride his cock as Logan took me from behind. I wanted to *be* Emily.

But I couldn't be. I was legally married to another man, a man named Jenkins, a man who had a lawful claim to me. I was still just a whore fucking two men who didn't know the truth. The fact that I didn't tell them, that I couldn't bring myself to tell them about my proxy marriage to Jenkins, made me worse than a whore. I wasn't just a whore; I was a liar, a selfish, spoiled liar who would do anything to feel the pleasure of their touch. Anything but tell them the truth, because the truth would end this dream for me. The truth would cost me everything.

Logan caressed my ass and kicked my ankles wider so my pussy was ripe and spread open for him. He teased me, inserting one long finger for just a moment before leaving me empty once more. "Tell us why Xander makes your face turn pink and your pussy wet, my Lizzie." Logan fucked me a bit harder, using two fingers and thrusting deep, leaving them buried inside me as he waited for my answer. "Tell us why watching him makes your pulse race and your breathing quicken."

What? How did he know? How could he know? "I don't—"

Smack.

"Ahhh! That hurt!" Logan had spanked my bottom with his free hand, hard. He pulled his fingers out and drove them deeper the second time. Spanked me again and again.

Smack.

Smack.

Smack.

"Do you want to fuck Xander?"

"No."

My pussy clenched at his words, a vivid image of Logan fucking me from behind as my dark hair fell forward on the bed. I didn't want Xander. I wanted to be like Emily, but I had no desire to be touched by her men.

I wanted my own.

"Your words say no, Lizzie, but your pussy says yes." Was that disappointment in his voice?

I tried to lift my head, but only managed to lift it far enough to catch Ford's worried expression. I *had* hurt their feelings. They thought I wanted another man. A married man! "No! That's not it at all. I don't want him to touch me. Never. I never wanted that."

Ford's eyes gentled, but the dark green depths still

held shadows. "Then tell us the truth, wife. What caused such a strong reaction in you?"

"I can't—" I shook my head and buried my face in the blankets as Logan pulled two fingers out, then fucked me with three.

"Is this what you want from Xander?"

The pleasure was exquisite and I felt my pussy flood with additional wetness to ease his way. "No."

"Tell me now."

"There's nothing to tell."

Logan's sigh was more a snarl of frustration and he spanked me hard and fast. I lost count of the number of times his hot palm made contact with my bare bottom, but as the sting faded into a liquid heat it spread through my body, making me feel warm and safe and numb. Maybe I should just tell them the truth. Maybe they wouldn't think poorly of me. They seemed kind and courteous to Emily and her men. And I hadn't spied on purpose.

"It was an accident!" Logan's hand stilled and I gathered my wits enough to speak, turning my tear-filled gaze to Ford. "I didn't mean to."

Ford's gaze was soft, patient. "Didn't mean to do what, love? You can tell us."

Logan hadn't taken his fingers out of my pussy while he spanked me, and the heat of his swats now felt like hot caramel that had melted and spread across my flesh to burrow deep into my core. I took a deep breath and blurted out the truth.

"I saw them, in Drummond, at the hotel. I saw them." I drew big, ragged gulps of air into my lungs, but Ford simply nodded. Logan stood behind me like a statue, waiting.

"Saw them what?"

"I saw them fucking in their hotel room." I scrunched my eyelids closed, hard, so I wouldn't have to see the look of disgust on Ford's face when I admitted the rest. "It was late. Really late and both of my sisters were already asleep. I heard a woman crying out and I thought she was in pain, so I…"

Ford lifted his hand from my shoulder and began to run a gentle finger along my cheek. "And what, love? You saw them fucking?"

"Yes."

"All three of them, naked and wild?" Logan's rough growl came from behind me and he moved his fingers in and out of me slowly as he spoke.

"Yes."

Logan's fingers pulled out fast, then plunged deep and I gasped. "And you liked it? Didn't you, Lizzie? It made you hot. It made you want to come. And when you look at Xander…" His voice trailed off and I opened my eyes to see Ford's frown.

"When she sees Xander, she can't get the image of him fucking Emily out of her mind."

Logan sighed. "I'm afraid that is a problem." He ran a fingertip over my clit and my gasp nearly caused me to miss his next question. "What was Xander doing to Emily, love?"

I shook my head, but he rubbed my clit again, then removed his soaking wet fingers to rub over the virgin rosette of my ass. "Was Xander taking her from behind?

Was his cock here?" As he spoke, Logan slowly pressed the tip of a finger into my virgin hole and I moaned. "Did you watch, Lizzie? Did you watch and imagine Xander was fucking you?"

I couldn't say it. I just couldn't.

Logan was relentless. He had a finger fully inside me now, the stretching and burning sensation was driving me to distraction, but I couldn't think, couldn't focus on a response because he fucked my pussy with his other hand, filling both holes at once. "Yes!"

I meant the word as a request, not an admission, but it served as both. Ford leaned over, his wicked voice in my ear as Logan left me for a moment, then returned, quickly. I could not see Logan, but I didn't need to. I could feel him, for within seconds both of his hands were where they had been before—invading my body with an expertise that made me dizzy.

Ford whispered, "Yes, you watched, didn't you? Did you like what they were doing to Emily? Did they take her together? Did they fill her up? Did you imagine yourself between two men, your husbands, as they both fucked you together?"

I groaned and pushed back against Logan's hands, unable to voice my desires.

"Keep talking, Ford, she likes it." Logan pulled his finger free of my ass and I felt a strange sensation, as if he were placing liquid or oil inside me. But he distracted me with his other hand on my clit and I had to focus to listen to Ford.

"Do you want us to fuck you like that, Lizzie? Do you want one of us to fill your pussy while the other puts a nice hard cock in your ass?" I bit my lip and he traced it with his finger as I opened my eyes to look at him. Pure, raw lust shone from his eyes into mine as he continued. "Because that's what we want, too."

"But first, you have to be ready." Logan spoke and I felt the round end of something hard probe my back entrance, hard, and a lot bigger then Logan's finger had been. I stiffened, but Ford shook his head and I froze.

"We've got to get you ready, love. Logan is going to put something inside that tight little arse of yours, something that will help you get ready for us."

I felt the invasion, slow and deliberate, as Logan pressed forward, then pulled back, twisting and working something hard and round into my ass. With a pop, I felt it slide past my inner muscles to settle deep within. Outside my body, a round object felt like it laid flat against my bottom.

"Good girl." I heard Logan drop his pants to the floor, but was still shocked when he grabbed my hips and pulled me backward, off the bed and onto his lap. I moaned in shock and need as I felt his hard cock probe my aching pussy. "Do you want me to fuck you now, Lizzie? Are you ready? Do you want to know what my cock will feel like with that nice, big plug shoved deep in your arse?"

The dirty talk made me squirm and I tried to impale myself on his hard length. He tsked, and locked his hands on my hips, holding me too high to get what I so desperately wanted. "No, love. No more denying the fire. You burn so nice and hot for us, and we love it. Don't we, Ford?"

My attention had been so completely focused on

Logan, that I missed Ford's movement. He was sitting on the edge of the bed, his cock on display, rising from his lap right in front of me. If I leaned forward, I could taste him as I'd tasted Logan last time. I wanted to know if he felt the same on my tongue, if he, too, was like the softest silk wrapped around steel.

Torn between my two desires, I lost track of what Logan had said to me. Ford grinned as he caught my eye. "I'm pretty sure she forgot the question, Logan. Better ask her again."

Logan obliged. "Do you want me to fuck you now, Lizzie?"

Damned to hell as I was for fucking two men who were not mine, I gave in to my base desires. Hell was hell. It couldn't get any worse. And I wanted my men, hot and rough and hard. "Yes. I want your cock, Logan." I licked my lips and met Ford's gaze. "But I want Ford's cock, too."

Ford threw his head back and laughed, but Logan lifted me and shifted us both forward several inches, until my head was directly above Ford's hard length.

"Suck on his cock, Lizzie. Deep, all the way to your throat, and I'll give you what you want." Logan's command made my blood sing and I eagerly lowered my head to Ford's cock, taking him deep and hard and fast, the way I knew would drive him crazy.

When I had taken him as deep as I could, his soft tip brushing the back of my throat, I started to pull back, but Ford's hands gripped my hair, only allowing me to lift off his cock enough to breathe as I felt Logan's cock breach my wet pussy, stretching me, filling me, too much. With the plug in my ass, his giant cock filled me too full, too wide, too big.

Logan's hips shifted and he pushed up, fucking me from behind, pushing and pushing until he was buried balls deep and my bare bottom rested against his thighs.

Logan stilled and Ford let me go. I lifted my mouth from his cock and raised my head to the ceiling, a soft cry escaping me. I was totally overwhelmed. I didn't know what to do.

Ford solved my problem. "Take my cock deep. Fuck me with your mouth the way you want Logan to fuck your pussy."

I lowered my lips to the crown of Ford's cock and Logan pulled out of me until just the top of him remained inside my wet heat. "That's all you want, little girl?"

No, that was *not* all.

I wrapped one hand around the base of Ford's cock and took him hard and fast, my mouth moving over him as fast and furious as I could take him in.

Behind me, Logan growled and fucked me the way I wanted, hard and fast.

Ford came first, his thick cum shooting down my throat as I kept moving on him.

When I released him, he lifted me, pulling me forward until my cheek rested on his chest, freeing Logan to fuck me harder and faster from behind.

With one long arm, Ford reached down beneath me and stroked my clit as Logan slammed into me over and over. The first orgasm rushed through me like a lightning strike, the pulsing spasms of my pussy walls all the more powerful because of the plug that filled my ass.

Logan slowed his pace, tilting his hips to hit a place inside me that made me come again before Logan finally filled me with his seed.

I collapsed when it was over. Logan left me and returned with a soft cloth he used to clean me, then brought me a drink, first a sip of whiskey, then cool water.

My caveman turned caretaker. He did not remove the butt plug. When I asked, Ford chuckled and said it was meant to prepare me to take both of them and needed to remain in me.

Since that was what I still wanted, I didn't argue.

When we were all cleaned up and settled in a big heap of snuggling bodies on the bed, my men wrapped themselves around me, and I slept.

CHAPTER 11

 *lizabeth*

EVER SINCE WE alighted from the stage in Hayes, my entire world had been turned upside-down. Perhaps it began when we left Omaha. Either way, this was the first time I felt in control of my life. It was silly really, but I was making pancakes. Pancakes and blueberry muffins, sliced ham, fried potatoes, scrambled eggs and a variety of other items for the morning meal.

We'd walked to Kane and Ian's house where we had dinner the night before and I'd asked if I could help make breakfast. A big man with a thick Scottish brogue named Connor all but dragged me into the kitchen. Anne and Emily were helping him, but they graciously accepted my assistance. Anne was a little distracted with her son, Christopher, who did not take to waiting very well. At

115

two, he sat at the kitchen table and had some sliced ham while the rest of the food cooked.

When I noticed the fire was a little high beneath the pancakes, Connor happily handed me his spatula. I'd been in front of the stove ever since, content.

"Don't forget the butter, Connor," I called over my shoulder.

"Did you used to run a boardinghouse?" Anne asked as she cut another piece of ham for Christopher.

"No. My uncle was very particular about his meals; all of the food had to be evenly hot."

Emily paused before taking a platter from a sideboard. She laughed. "The men here only care that it's tasty and plentiful."

"Aye. We are not verra picky," Connor added.

I stirred the potatoes, then added another dollop of lard to the pan.

"You seem to have adjusted well to becoming a bride," Anne offered, a sly smile on her lips.

I turned pink, but it hopefully was hidden by the heat of the stove.

"I heard you were to marry a mean man and that Logan and Ford saved you."

Her words made my stomach sour. I'd forgotten, what with being spanked and fucked and plugged and all, about the proxy marriage letter. Ford and Logan had saved me, but I was actually married to Mr. Jenkins.

"Yes, from what they said, he was going to share me with his sons."

"That's nay what your men are doing with you," Connor said. He leaned a hip against the sideboard and crossed his arms. "Giving you to his grown sons is akin to rape. Logan and Ford *married* you. While not legally for both of them, but Logan sees Ford's name as his in that church ledger."

I swallowed at the vehemence of his words. "I know."

"Are you all right then, with everything they do to you?" Emily asked, her voice low, but with the way the corner of Connor's mouth turned up, he heard just the same.

This time none of them could miss the hot blush on my cheeks. I delayed an answer by scooping up the crispy potatoes into a bowl. Connor came over and took it from me, carried it into the dining room. I waited until he was gone to speak.

"Emily, I… I have a confession." Ford and Logan had shown me that I shouldn't be ashamed of my feelings. Watching Emily and her men that night had, in a strange way, set me free. I was no longer ashamed of it, but I felt I needed to let her know why I'd been acting so strangely.

"Oh?" she asked. She took a pitcher of water from the pump sink and gave it to Connor when he came back in. Taking the hint, he turned around and left once again.

"I… um, I saw you, in Drummond."

"That's all right. But now I feel badly that I didn't say hello. You must have been terrified to come here. I could have talked to you about it. Helped." She was so nice, so thoughtful and yet I knew she liked her men to pull on her hair and fuck her hard. I glanced away.

"No, I mean, I saw you in your hotel room late that night. With Xander and Tyler." I bit my lip, then took a deep breath. "I didn't know who you were back then. I

117

was in the room next door. I thought you were in pain. I got up to help, went out onto the balcony, and saw you all —together." I exhaled and turned back to the potatoes.

She was quiet for a minute, yet Anne was laughing.

Emily tilted her head to look at me as if I were truly odd. "That's why you're petrified of Xander?"

"I'm not petrified. I'm just embarrassed, really. I should have turned away, once I figured it out. But you were so— I mean, I saw you… well, you know." I spoke to the potatoes, not Emily.

"If I remember correctly, oh God, yes, that was a very good night." She leaned over, inserting her face between mine and the potatoes so I would have to look at her. "They took me together that night. Have your men truly shared you yet?"

"It's too soon. They have to prepare her first," Anne said, coming up to stand on the other side of me. Her words brought to mind the large plug Logan had placed in my ass the day before. I felt stretched and slightly sore, but that was all. If it meant I could have what Emily had— well, I wasn't going to say no.

Emily took my silence for shame and tried to ease my mind. "Don't be embarrassed. Bridgewater men are different. They are more dominant and demanding—"

"Caring."

"Possessive."

"Rugged."

Emily ran her hands up over her abdomen and slid them, shamelessly, over her full breasts as if remembering her lovers' touch. "Our men are more virile than others. Trust me, I was married before and I know. Perhaps it was because they've been to war. Perhaps because of the customs of Mohamir. Maybe their fucking is so intense because it's always two of them claiming you at once. I don't know the reason, and I don't care. With my husbands, I always come first."

Anne laughed. "Usually more than once." She began to lift the bacon from a frying pan with a long, sharp fork. "Rebecca will have to tell you about the time Connor and Dash dragged her away from the lunch table and fucked her over Kane's desk while the rest of them finished their meal."

I know my jaw dropped, but I closed it quickly and looked at Anne to see if her words were a jest. They weren't and I blushed at the thought of Ford and Logan fucking me, making me cry out and beg while an entire table full of people finished a meal in the next room.

The thoughts were a distraction I did not need, so I focused on scooping the potatoes into a bowl Emily handed to me before they burned.

"Ach, we did at that," Connor said, coming in and taking the filled bowl. He winked at me with a sly grin. "Anne, I believe, was so needy one day that her men spanked her and then fucked her in the living room during dinner."

Anne did flush then, but she smiled as she thought about it. "My milk had come in and I was tired and fretful and needy. Andrew and Robert knew what I needed."

"A good orgasm—or three," Emily said, then burst out laughing.

I was stunned by their casual approach to fucking. It was not kept behind closed doors and the men didn't treat the women as whores to be fucked and used, but as their cherished brides. It was how Logan and Ford made me feel: cherished. Special. Adored.

It was then that Logan stuck his head into the kitchen. "Everything all right in here?" he asked, clearly checking on me. Heat spread through my chest at the sight of him, and it had nothing to do with lust, and everything to do with a strange new feeling I wasn't ready to face yet.

"I'm fine, Logan. Thank you."

He entered the kitchen with a grin before leaning down to kiss my temple, his heart in his eyes. I felt a longing then, a happiness at seeing him that surprised me, and I smiled back, leaning into his gentle touch.

"Your wife is learning all about Bridgewater men and their... expectations during dinner." Connor slapped Logan on the back as he carried the platter of ham away.

Emily lifted her hands to her hips and raised a brow, looking every bit like an angry schoolteacher as she spoke to Logan. "Lizzie was telling us that you are neglecting her training, not satisfying *all* of her needs."

"What?" I sputtered, seeing Emily's eyes fill with the very devil as Anne burst out laughing. "I said no such thing."

Logan arched one dark brow. "Is that so?"

"It is," Emily confirmed.

"Anne, please go tell Ford that our wife needs tending," Logan said. He came over to me and took my hand, leading me to the back door, which was open to let the heat out. "Emily, will you finish plating the rest of the food with Connor?"

I eyed her with fake anger. "Emily!" I cried.

Her grin was infectious, but I was too nervous to return it now. She had the nerve to wink at me as Logan pulled me to the door. "We'll be even after this, Lizzie, although I doubt your men will let me watch."

I sputtered as Logan pushed me out onto the back porch.

"Now wife, you feel as if your men have been neglecting you?"

I shook my head and backed up until my bottom hit the porch railing.

I wasn't afraid of him, for he was grinning amiably. I *was* afraid of what he was going to do to me right there on Kane's back porch.

"No, I'm fine."

Ford appeared from where he'd been, waiting at the breakfast table. He stepped out onto the porch to stand beside Logan.

"It's been a whole hour since we played with that arse of yours and pulled the plug free," Logan continued, not sparing Ford a glance. "Perhaps we need to put the next size up in you now, let you think about how well your men take care of you all through breakfast."

Ford pulled a plug from his shirt pocket and held it up.

"You kept that in your pocket?" I asked incredulously.

He shrugged unabashedly. "We are always ready to take care of you, sweetheart. We want to take you together and you need to be prepared for it. It was only a matter of time before we pulled you aside to fill you up again."

Ford turned around and reached into the kitchen to grab a jar from a shelf on the wall. It was the same slick ointment they'd used on me in the cabin the night before. Kane and Ian kept it on the kitchen shelf? Out in the open?

"Face the railing, lift your skirts and bend over. If you're a good girl, we'll fuck you after breakfast."

"Everyone in the dining room will know!" I shouted, then bit my lip.

"Sweetheart, they already know your husbands are taking care of you. You might as well get some pleasure out of it."

Both waited patiently and watched me, their dark brows raised in the same questioning look. Would I obey them or defy them? Would I accept their pleasure? Would I accept them?

I took a deep breath, then another, then turned around and began to lift the hem of my dress. With my ass on display, I kept my eyes closed as my men first added the slick lubricant to my back entrance, working plenty of it deep inside me before working the bigger plug in. I tried to conjure up the old feelings of humiliation and guilt, but I simply could not find the shame or self-loathing I once wore like an old familiar coat. Submitting to their touch gave my men pleasure. I gave them pleasure, and I refused to feel bad about that.

And they were my men. I might not be legally married to them, but they were mine. A darkly possessive beast rose to the surface as I felt them play with my ass. I started to pant through their ministrations, my fingers gripping the railing. They were mine, not in the eyes of the law, but in their eyes and mine, and as far as I was concerned, we were the only people who counted.

Perhaps I'd get lucky, and simply never see Mr. Jenkins again as long as I lived. That would be a fine solution, and this ranch was several days' ride from Hayes. I would keep my new husbands, and no one would ever have to know the truth.

As I sat through breakfast with Ford on my right, Logan on my left, and a very large reminder of their claim on both my heart and my body deep in my bottom, I accepted the truth. I had fallen in love with my husbands, and if I had to lie to keep them, I would. Forever.

CHAPTER 12

$\mathcal{L}$*ogan*

A BUSY WEEK passed and we quickly learned how much land Bridgewater had. With fall approaching, we had to bring the herd in from distant grazing land, repair fences, prepare for the harvest of wheat and hay. Closer to the houses, the large garden was producing vegetables and fruit that needed to be canned. Everyone was busy. Never in my wildest dreams did I expect to become an American cowboy. Growing up in Manchester, I lived two lives, one of relative comfort and safety while my father was alive. I'd been a merchant's son, going to school. I'd learned reading and my maths, and felt like the world was full of wondrous possibilities. Then my father died, and my mother was left destitute. We lost our home and I took to the streets to try to steal enough food to keep us both alive.

She died after a few years. I was too old to go back to school, and too dirty to do much else. I sold my mother's wedding band to buy my conscription into the military. Mohamir's way of life seemed so much smarter, safer, and saner than the suffering I'd seen on the streets.

Now I finally had my bride, but she was holding back. I could sense it. Ford knew it, too, but we couldn't figure out how to make Lizzie open up. We fucked her senseless, cared for her and kept her safe. Spanking her could force her to share her problems, but she liked it too much. Besides, we wanted her to learn she could come to us.

Ford advised patience, but that was such a nobleman's game. He'd played the political game at court, learning at the feet of one of the greatest manipulators of all time, his father, the marquess.

However, his father also donated his seed to several mistresses, producing a string of bastard sons eager to see Ford dead. After the third attempt on his life, Ford had told his father to sod off and joined the military.

There was no going back, not for either of us. Nor did we want to. The wide open prairie was amazing and different, the mountains in the distance the biggest things I'd ever seen. Nothing compared to the sunsets in the territory, not even the desert glow in Mohamir. It was an incredible feeling to know that after such a long journey, so many miles, that we were finally home. Home with Lizzie.

She, too, seemed to thrive at Bridgewater. Her struggles with her bloody uncle's verbal abuse had taken a harsh toll, but Ford and I were working with her on it. While she always loved how we fucked her, she was becoming more relaxed about it, even joking and teasing the other women about how we Bridgewater men were primitive, cave-dwelling creatures who did nothing more than throw our women over our shoulders and fuck them like mindless animals.

I had to admit, when I had Lizzie naked and spread open before me, her pussy glistening with proof of her desire, and the world *please* on her lips… aye, I was a bit of a caveman then.

She was passionate in bed play, she did behave like a wanton. She did like to watch others fucking. She had a wild creature inside her as well, one that loved it when I fucked her hard and deep, one that loved the strong pull of a man's mouth on her clit. At our first touch, her body melted with desire, in complete submission to our needs. That made her perfect for us.

Ford had dragged her into the tack room and fucked her up against the wall. She'd learned to suck cock by the edge of the creek, her knees in the soft grass. She'd taken the larger and larger plugs in her ass, knowing we'd soon claim her together. Each and every time we ensured she came at least once, often twice.

When we weren't fucking her, we were working. This morning, Lizzie was in the barn, learning how to tend to a new foal born the night before. Ford and I were moving a small herd of twenty head of cattle up to the main pasture behind the house when Emma ran out to the fence, little Christopher in her arms. She looked upset, and I kicked my horse in the sides to get the ornery stallion to move a bit faster. I pulled up on the reins, hard, and the horse's sides brushed the sides of the fence a few feet from where she stood.

Emma waited for Ford to join us seconds later, then surprised us both.

"The sheriff's here and he's asking for Lizzie."

ELIZABETH

"DON'T WORRY, Lizzie. You've done nothing wrong, so there's nothing to fear," Logan murmured, guiding me toward Kane and Ian's house with a hand at the small of my back.

I felt as if I would vomit. I knew why he was here. He was here to take me to Mr. Jenkins, my true husband, the man to whom I was actually married. The wedding to Ford, while it had been in a church, couldn't be legal since I was already wed to another at the time I took my vows. I'd been living in the worst sort of sin ever since. Both Ford and Logan had been correct. My uncle's words were untrue. I wasn't tainted. I was passionate and loved what they did to me, even when they put those dreaded plugs in my bottom. I knew it was for my own good, for they'd soon fuck me together. No, not any longer. I'd be leaving with the sheriff and returning to Hayes.

A lump of fear lodged in my throat and I couldn't respond to Logan's reassuring words. Ford came running from the barn along with Ian and Brody.

When he walked alongside of us, he removed his hat

and wiped his brow. "What's this about the sheriff?" he asked. His sleeves on his shirt were rolled up, showing off his corded muscles. His blunt fingers gently held his hat, just as he'd used them to touch me in such wonderful, remarkable ways. No longer.

"Don't know," Logan replied. He opened the front door and we walked through the house to the kitchen where we heard voices. This was the moment I'd been dreading, when the men—everyone—would learn the truth.

The sheriff was a large man, with broad shoulders and a barrel chest. He had white hair that had thinned and his pale scalp glistened. He was smiling at something Emma was telling him as he held a cup of steaming coffee.

The smells of breakfast lingered and it only added to my nausea.

When we entered, the sheriff stood.

"Brody, good to see you. How's Laurel?" he asked. It seemed the sheriff was familiar and relaxed with those at Bridgewater.

"Well, thank you."

"Her father and Mr. Palmer were quite the duo, but I'm glad you prevailed."

I didn't know about what he spoke, but it sounded as if it had to do with Laurel, his wife with Mason.

"Thank you," Brody offered.

The sheriff turned to me then, pleasantries out of the way and looked me over in a professional way. "Ma'am," he said. "I assume you are Elizabeth Lewis?"

I could only nod. Gripping my hands together, I tried to hide the fact that they were shaking.

"You're scaring our bride, sheriff," Logan said, pulling me into his side and kissing my temple. I closed my eyes at the gentle touch.

"I don't mean anything of the sort. I'll get to the point of my visit." His eyes shifted from Logan to me. "I have been asked to find a missing woman, one Elizabeth Lewis, who was supposed to arrive in Hayes via the stage from Omaha."

"That's Lizzie."

The sheriff glanced at Ford when he answered for me, then back at me.

"There's a Mr. Samuel Jenkins who is concerned about you. Says he paid your fare from Omaha and has no bride to show for it."

I bit my lip and looked at the floor.

"That's no fault of hers, sheriff," Ford said. "Have you met Jenkins?"

"Can't say that I've had the pleasure," he replied. "I received a telegram from the sheriff in Hayes about the matter."

"The man's a bloody bastard, ready to share Lizzie with his two grown sons."

The sheriff's eyebrows went up as he clenched his jaw.

"We saved her from him and Ford here—" Logan tilted his head in Ford's direction, "—married Lizzie in the Hayes church."

"Legally?"

Ford nodded. "Yes, sir."

"No, you didn't." The words fell from my mouth; the guilt and pressure at keeping them in was too much.

Everyone looked to me. Emma gasped. Brody crossed

his arms over his chest. Logan and Ford stared at me wide-eyed.

"Explain, ma'am."

I couldn't look at them any longer and glanced down at the wood floor. "I have a proxy marriage with Mr. Jenkins. It was completed in Omaha the morning I left. When Ford married me, he was pretending to be Jenkins. I would have refused him otherwise."

I paused then, but didn't lift my head. All was quiet in the house and they were all waiting for me.

"I didn't realize I was married to someone other than Mr. Jenkins until Ford told me the truth about who he was—after we were married. I never meant to commit bigamy."

Logan forced my chin up. "You've been keeping this secret all this time?"

He became blurry when tears filled my eyes. I could only nod the slightest bit. "I was afraid to get rid of it. It's a legal document. I wasn't sure what would happen to me. I didn't know what to do."

"Where's this proxy letter now?" the sheriff asked.

I couldn't turn my head to look at him, but said, "In my bag. Buried at the bottom."

"I'd like to see it, please."

Brody responded. "I'll go."

I heard his footsteps down the hall, then the door close behind him.

I had no idea how long it took for him to return. Five, ten minutes perhaps, but they were the longest of my life. Logan released my chin and began pacing. Ford looked at me, but his gaze wasn't filled with any of the warmth to which I was accustomed. Emma offered me a small smile, but when a baby's cries came from overhead, she excused herself and went upstairs to tend to Ellie.

The sheriff thankfully remained silent and drank his coffee.

When the front door opened once again, I jumped. Brody returned and handed the slip of paper to the sheriff. He unfolded it and took his time reading it. There wasn't much, a simple document with a seal that married me to Mr. Samuel Jenkins.

When finished, the sheriff looked at me. "Tell me, ma'am. Who do you want for a husband? Ford here?" He flicked his gaze to Ford. "Or Mr. Jenkins?"

I licked my lips and looked at both my men. "I want Ford." There was no hesitation. I wanted him. I wanted Logan. "That's just a piece of paper. A paper that means I'm legally tied to another, but it doesn't show what I feel for Ford. I consider him my husband."

"All right then."

I whipped my head about and frowned at the sheriff.

He took another sip of his coffee. "You see, ma'am, this proxy letter is for *your* own good. When a woman travels across the country to marry a stranger, a proxy letter protects her from a man changing his mind. There's nothing worse—and I've seen a few—than a woman arriving on the stage and her intended takes one look at her and changes his mind. She has no money, no way to return home. She's stranded and destitute and often forced to work in less than *savory* of conditions."

I understood what he was saying. The idea of being

rejected had crossed my mind the entire ride from Omaha.

The sheriff shrugged. "I've seen a dozen just like this. A judge in these parts will force the marriage, but only at the woman's insistence. I would bet fifty dollars Mr. Jenkins knows nothing of this paper."

My eyes widened. "I beg your pardon?" I whispered.

"He told me to find a woman named Elizabeth Lewis, not his wife. He doesn't know you were married by proxy. All he knows is you didn't show up when you were supposed to, and this bunch..." the sheriff pointed at Logan, Ford and other men in the room, "...was passing through town and he saw them with some pretty ladies."

"I don't understand." My heart beat too fast, like a hummingbird and I couldn't process what the sheriff was saying. It was too good to be true. "What does that mean?"

"Do you want Ford?" he asked, instead of answering my question.

"Yes," I replied, tilting my chin up.

The sheriff smiled and handed the document back to me. "As a man sworn to uphold the letter of the law, I can't do anything about your predicament. You, however, have the power to solve this problem yourself."

Confused, I reached out and accepted the marriage document, staring at the sheriff like he'd grown two heads. "I don't understand."

With a twinkle in his eye, he walked over to the side of the room where a small log fire burned low on the grate, just enough to keep the morning chill out of the room. His gaze lingered on the fire, moved to the letter in my hands, and then rose to meet my startled gaze, his eyebrow raised as if I should be able to read his mind.

The fire crackled and popped, a log breaking in two as embers flew into the air in a spray of glowing orange sparks. My mouth fell open as I realized what he was telling me. If Mr. Jenkins didn't know the proxy letter existed, then this very fragile, very flammable piece of paper in my hand was the only evidence, anywhere, that I had signed my name and agreed to accept him as my husband. If what the sheriff said was true, there would be no record at all, not in any township or courthouse, not in a single church or law office.

"Unless Mr. Jenkins decides to take a gander at the church ledger in town, which, based on what I've been told about him, will never happen, he'll never know you arrived in Hayes at all, let alone married someone else." The sheriff cleared his throat and stepped back, away from the fireplace, giving me plenty of room to get closer.

"Even if he did head into that church, Lizzie is mine," Ford added, his eyes holding mine in a stare I'd come to recognize, the gaze he used when he was making me a promise. As I'd learned over the last few days, when he made his wife a vow, he kept his word. Ford spoke loud enough for everyone in the room to hear him, but I knew he was only speaking to me. "Jenkins can scream all he likes, but I signed my full, legal name in that church ledger. Lizzie is my wife in the eyes of God and the church. And I'm not going to give her up."

I crumbled the marriage paper between my palms, rolling it into a nice ball as the sheriff crossed his arms over his chest with a grin. "What God has joined together, let no man put asunder. I believe those are the proper words."

I smiled, too, the force of it stretching my cheeks until they stung as I took three steps and tossed the marriage document onto the fire. As the edges turned back and curled in on themselves, I watched with an intensity I could barely contain. I needed that paper to burn, to become the smallest flakes of ash scattered like dust under the flames.

Logan knelt down next to the grate with a hint of mischief in his eyes and blew softly until the paper caught fire, burning hot and fast until it was completely engulfed in dancing orange and gold flames.

The sheriff slapped his hand on Ford's back. "Guess that takes care of that. I got a message for you and Logan from the rest of your boys. Someone by the name of Garrett."

Ford nodded. "He's with me. What's the message?"

The sheriff grinned. "Seems he's been delayed. Got himself hitched to a beautiful little thing, named Rebekah. Said they were all running a bit late, but to let you know they were all safe and sound." I gasped, shocked at the news that Garrett had married my little sister! And with who? I knew these men, knew how they thought. Rebekah didn't have just one husband now, but two. "What about my sister Judith, sheriff? Did Garrett say anything about her?"

"Nope. Just Rebekah. Sorry I don't have more news. Garrett said they'll be arriving in a day or two." With a congenial grin, he nodded to everyone in the room and bowed to me. "I'll be heading back to town, Mrs. Ellison, unless there's anything else I can do for you?"

"No, thank you, sheriff." I bowed my head in gratitude to him, but he just laughed. His gaze was warm and friendly, and I forced myself to turn away from the sight of the final remnants of paper turning black when he spoke. "I guess I'll have to inform poor Mr. Jenkins that there's no sign of his intended bride up in these parts."

With that, he nodded at Ian, put his hat back on his head and walked out of the house.

Mrs. Ellison! I was free!

Ford and Logan surrounded me, holding me between them where I felt safe and cherished and very loved. I heard the others scatter to give us privacy. When I knew we were alone, I felt myself begin to tremble, the shock of the sheriff's arrival and the events of the past few minutes finally catching up to my body. It felt so good to be in their arms, to feel the press of their hard bodies, to breathe in their scents, to know I was truly theirs, forever.

They held me in silence for several minutes, but I felt Logan's growing impatience in the hard planes of his body and I knew I was in trouble. Ford's words confirmed it. "Wife, I believe there are some things we need to discuss."

"Yes, there are." Logan added, nearly growling in my ear from behind me. "Lying, Lizzie? Keeping secrets from your husbands?"

I stiffened as Logan pulled away from me and I tried to defend my actions. I looked up into Ford's eyes, hoping that at least he, as the more emotionally controlled man in my life, would try to understand my side of the story. "I didn't know what to do. I was scared."

"I know. And so does Logan. But you should have told us of the situation. We know what's best for you. You are our top priority. All this time you spent worried and upset about that worthless piece of paper when your only thoughts should have been on your husbands and how to build a new life here, with us. That document was a threat to all of us, yet you chose to keep it to yourself. You should have trusted us to take care of you." Ford took my hand and led me out of the house as we followed Logan across the grass toward our much smaller home.

My nerves sizzled with awareness. I couldn't keep my eyes from the tense lines of Logan's broad shoulders. Nor could my mind make sense of the difference between Ford's gentle tone of voice and iron strength of his grip. I was free from Mr. Jenkins, forever. Shouldn't that make them happy? I was nearly giddy with relief, but I knew Ford was right. If I had shown them the paper, it would have been destroyed already, and no threat to us. What if the sheriff had been on Mr. Jenkins' side of the argument? Or had no love for Ford?

Ashamed with myself, I worried what my men were going to do to punish me. I knew they wouldn't truly hurt me, but the tense line of Ford's jaw did not make me eager to learn what they had in mind. Once we were far enough away from the main house not to be overheard, I asked, "Where are you taking me?"

Ford didn't look at me as he picked up the pace. I was practically running to keep up with his agitated stride. Logan was even farther ahead.

"You lied to us, Lizzie."

"I'm sorry." And I was. I truly was. I could tell my lack of trust in them had hurt them more deeply than I cared to admit. They'd done nothing but take care of me and protect me from the moment they'd seen me. I should have trusted them. Why could I so easily give them my body, but not surrender my heart? Why was I still holding back?

If I had truly fallen in love with them, I would have told them everything. I would have laid my ear over Ford's beating heart and told him how scared I was. I would have held tightly to Logan and trusted my warriors to defeat my enemy. But I'd kept that part of myself from them. I hadn't surrendered everything, and now they both knew it.

Ford shook his head. "Sorry isn't good enough, sweetheart. Not this time."

CHAPTER 13

I WANTED to take my wife over my knee and spank her until she couldn't sit down for a week. I wanted to fuck her so hard she'd never get me out of her body. I wanted to hold her down until she screamed, and sobbed, and told me why she'd kept this secret from us, why she still didn't trust us to take care of her.

If I were honest, most of the anger churning within was self-directed. Logan and I had the most beautiful, most sensual, kind-hearted and loving woman for a wife, and she did not love us, did not trust us.

We'd failed her somehow. As I pulled her along to the privacy of our small home, I tried to figure out what to do next. We'd spanked her, fucked her, and cherished her. She slept nestled between us every night, safe and warm and surrounded by two men who would die to protect her.

It wasn't enough. We'd conquered her body, but we hadn't overcome her fears, hadn't been able to win her heart.

We reached the house and Logan left the door open, as he was already inside. Lizzie glanced up at me, a cloud of tears gathering in her eyes, but I shook my head. No, I was not going to let her go. Not now. Not ever.

I did not force her across the threshold; this had to be her decision. I would never force her to accept us. Hell, if I could force her to love us, I would, but that had already proven impossible.

In the rational part of my mind, I knew that we expected a lot from her. We'd only known her for a short time. Love often took months or years to grow.

But I was a greedy bastard, I wanted it now. So did Logan.

I could live without her love, for now, but I could not survive with my mind intact without her trust.

Lizzie squared her shoulders and stepped inside our house. I followed her immediately, squinting blindly for a few seconds as my eyes adjusted to the dimly lit interior after walking in such bright sunlight.

"Close the door, Ford." Logan's voice drifted to us both from a dark corner of the room and I kicked the door closed with my foot, not wanting to take my eyes off our bride, not for a single second. I had no idea what she was going to do.

Silence built in the small room as I waited to see what Logan intended. I knew he was struggling, too, for the quiet went long, growing until it was more painful to my ears than a cannon shot on the battlefield.

The stakes were higher here than on any battlefield we'd ever set foot on. There, I simply risked my life. Here, with Lizzie, I risked my future, my heart and soul. They were hers, had been since the first moment I set eyes on her when she climbed down out of that stagecoach.

Logan held himself perfectly still, waiting, for God only knew what. To my surprise, Lizzie spoke first.

"I'm truly sorry, husbands. I should have told you everything. I put our family in danger. I was foolish and scared, and I should have trusted you with the truth as easily as I trust you with my body." She walked forward, into the center of the room, and began to unfasten the buttons of her dress.

I watched, spellbound, eager to see her naked form, even as disbelief warred with the eager surge of my cock. We'd taken Lizzie's pleasure many times, but she had never initiated our loving, never offered herself to us first. Not once.

Her dress dropped to a pool around her feet, followed by her corset—no drawers for her were allowed—until she stood naked and beautiful in the center of the room. She walked to the bed, head high like a queen's, and crawled to the center, kneeling there, she faced us with her hands on her lap and her head bowed, waiting for whatever we chose to do. The long, elegant lines of her body was like a sculptor's art, the curve of her hips so perfectly formed that I longed to grab those hips and hold on tight as I rammed my cock deep.

Logan stepped forward as if under a spell, stopping to

look at me. I met his gaze; mine, I was sure, was filled with as much surprise as his. I had expected Logan to throw her over his knee and spank her until she cried. I had expected her to yell at us, to plead, to fight us with words and, if necessary, fists and feet. After that, we would have seduced her with hands and tongue, fucked her until she screamed her release, until she couldn't see straight, then slept with her cradled in our arms.

But this offering? Her complete and total surrender?

I knew I was supposed to feel like the conquering hero, but seeing her there, bared to us and offering us everything, I felt like the conquered. Her surrender brought me to my knees.

Logan reached for the hem of his shirt, yanking it off over his head in one smooth motion. I followed suit, and soon we raced to be naked, next to her. Inside her. It was time to claim our bride, to fuck her together, as we'd longed to do for days. After, she would never doubt exactly whom she belonged to again.

ELIZABETH

"WHAT ARE YOU DOING, LIZZIE?" Ford asked, but he was undressing, baring his body as Logan had already done. They stood at the foot of the bed gloriously naked, their cocks huge and hard, and I wanted them both. While Logan stood before me with his arms braced on his hips, Ford crossed his arms instead, not yet ready to trust me. The gesture did not indicate he was going to be fucking me anytime soon. It also seemed that neither would be spanking me.

I swallowed down my nerves so I could answer him. I'd thought my motives obvious. "I'm... I'm giving myself to you, completely. To both of you."

His dark brow winged up. "Why?"

I frowned and lifted my head to meet his gaze. "Why?" I repeated.

"Why are you giving yourself to us?" His dark green eyes held doubts, ghosts that I'd placed there with my secrets, my lies. The sight nearly broke me all over again. I could not stand the thought that I'd caused these two men, my men, pain.

"Because... because I... I love you." The admission ripped my heart open. I was bare to them now, body and soul. I'd given them my body in the week we'd been married, but I hadn't given them my love. Now, now I was ready to give them everything.

Silence settled, thick and heavy in the room, my ragged breathing the only sound that reached my ears as I looked from Logan's fierce expression to Ford's unreadable face. Logan looked like he wanted to fuck me raw, punish me with his cock and his body until I surrendered completely. Ford, however, scared me more. Passion I could understand, but Ford's coldness demanded more from me; he wouldn't be satisfied with physical surrender. He would demand my mind and my soul. Logan would make me scream with pleasure, but Ford? Ford would deny me, Ford would make me beg.

My pussy grew wet as my thoughts chased each other around and around in my mind. I wanted both. I wanted them both, so much. I looked Logan in the eye, so he would know I spoke from the depths of my soul. "I love you, Logan. Your love is fierce and wild and you push me to take risks. You make me feel safe and loved, you let me be myself."

I turned to Ford, my hands twisting in my lap as I looked at him, refusing to blink. "I love you, Ford. You seduce me with your words, you force me to face the truth, to see the world in new ways. You are the calm to Logan's storm." I looked down at my hands, unable to face the intensity of their stares or their silence for another moment. "When I'm between you, when you touch me, I feel like you love me, like the world is a perfect place, like I am perfect."

Ford's arms dropped to his sides and he sighed. "You are perfect, sweetheart." He took a step forward and I raised my chin to look at him. "And we do love you. More than you know."

"We're going to fuck you now. Together," Logan told me. "Do you know why?" he asked.

"Because I belong to both of you."

"That's right, love. You're the one who makes us a family, who holds us together. You're the center of our world. We're going to have you between us, fuck you together. Then you'll know Ford and I both love you. Both cherish you. Both take care of your every need."

Logan's words were like a balm to my weakened confidence and relief was like a tidal wave that threatened to topple me from my place on the bed. They weren't angry any longer. We were going to be a family forever.

Ford's next words caused my heart to speed behind my

ribs. "You hold all the power, Lizzie. We might dominate you in bed, but you're the only one who can bring us to our knees. When I heard about the proxy letter, that you were really married to that bloody arsehole, I saw red."

"You chose us when you burned that piece of paper, and you'll take both of our cocks," Logan stepped forward and settled his knee on the edge of the bed, already pushing my boundaries, always challenging me, "...right now."

CHAPTER 14

lizabeth

I NODDED, trying not to stare at the two large cocks nearly within reach. "Yes. I want both of you. Together."

I knew what this meant. I knew that one of them would fill my pussy while the other filled my bottom with their cocks. They'd been preparing me, stretching me wider and wider with those plugs for just this moment. While I'd resisted their efforts before, now I understood why the plugs had been necessary. My men were being gentle, preparing me, for they wanted our final consummation to be perfect. It would be. With Logan and Ford it couldn't be anything else.

For the first time since I'd seen Emily with her men that night on the balcony, I wasn't jealous of the passion I'd witnessed. That wild love was mine now, with these two men, my husbands. Mine. I didn't need to envy another woman when the two sexiest men on the planet were naked and moving toward me.

I licked my lips at the idea of sucking one or both of their cocks deep into my mouth. I stretched, lifting my arms over my head and I watched with satisfaction as my lovers' eyes shifted to my swaying breasts, to the juncture of my thighs.

I felt so small kneeling in front of Ford, so feminine. With each breath, I studied the broad expanse of his chest. Dark hair tickled my fingers and I leaned in to brush my lips over the soft skin. For a man so powerful and virile, his skin was incredibly warm and smooth. As I moved closer, his hard cock jutted out and nudged my belly.

Glancing up at him, I saw the way his eyes had darkened. He was aroused, but he had yet to touch me. I knew he needed more than words, more than my simple declaration of love. I knew he wanted me to tend to him, to show him how much I longed to have him join the three of us. Together.

Dropping down onto my hands and knees, I turned as Logan knelt on the bed next to Ford. Two large cocks were directly before me. Ford's was thick and long, the dark crown red and eager. A pearly drop of fluid seeped from the slit in the middle. Logan's was just as impressive, but he stroked it as I watched.

"Show us, love," Logan said, his voice rough. "Prove you are ready to belong to both of us."

The way the men looked down at me, with arousal keen in their faces and in every hard line of their bodies, I could feel my nipples harden. I was between them, right where I wanted to be. I was sheltered, protected. Cherished. I knelt before them and I wanted to worship them both.

I took Ford's cock in my hand in the tight grip he'd shown me and with a flick of my tongue, licked away his salty essence. He growled as I swirled my tongue around, then took him deep. He was silky soft and tasted divine. I closed my eyes and settled in to my task, pleasuring him.

When his hands tangled in my hair, I knew he was correct. I did hold power over him. I was the only one who could make him this desperate, out of control and needy. I was the only one to give him the pleasure his body desired. To fulfill every one of his carnal needs.

"Don't forget Logan," Ford murmured.

With one last suck, I pulled off Ford and swiveled to take Logan's cock deep. He still held the base and I braced my hands on his muscled thighs for balance.

I had no idea how long I went from one to the other, pleasuring them, tasting their fluid as it painted my tongue.

"Enough," Logan growled. I pulled back and looked up at him through lowered lashes. I'd pushed them close to the brink.

Dropping to the edge of the bed, he held out his hand and I took it, letting him help me to my feet. He spun me about to face away from him. "Show Ford what's his."

Tipping up my chin, I met Ford's gaze, but he wasn't looking at my face, but my body. Rolling my shoulders back, I thrust my breasts out for him to see. His nostrils flared at the sight and I lifted my hands to cup each one, making sure my pebbled nipples stuck out in invitation.

Hooking an arm about my waist, Logan pulled me back so I was directly in front of him, then walked us both forward until my thighs met the edge of the bed. I stood directly in front of Ford, his eyes devouring me, tracing my body with his gaze when I wanted his tongue.

With one large hand, Logan found his way up my belly to take a breast, playing with the nipple. My hands fell away at the sharp feel of his teasing and I dropped my head back onto his shoulder, giving them complete access to my body.

While Logan played with my nipple, Ford reached forward, his fingers diving into my hot, wet core. "She's dripping," he growled.

Ford's eyes flared as he replaced one finger with two. I moaned and pushed against his hand, eager to feel his touch on my clit.

"She likes to suck her men's cocks." Fingers deep in my pussy, Ford leaned forward, taking the nipple Logan held for him deep into his mouth.

I did love their cocks, but I couldn't reply. Pressed between them, my mind had given up the sound of words. All I could do was feel.

"Do you think she will like our cocks filling her holes?" Behind me, Logan lowered his hand to trace the curve of my ass before moving lower, gathering a bit of my wet pussy juices on his fingers. They both stretched me, Ford from the front, and Logan from behind, filling me nearly as full as they did with their huge cocks.

With a growl in my ear that meant he was on the edge of losing control. Logan abandoned my pussy lips to explore my back entrance with his wet finger. He didn't play, but quickly worked a finger into me.

I breathed deep at the feel of him penetrating me there.

Ford lifted his head from my breast, but left his fingers deep in my pussy. I had one of my men filling each hole already, and I was about to beg them to fuck me. I needed them to fuck me, to fill me up and make me theirs forever. I wanted to come all over their cocks, squeezing them, milking them with both of their hard lengths buried deep inside me.

Without breaking eye contact, Ford reached for the jar of ointment on the dresser. He held it up and Logan released my breast to twist off the lid.

Logan dipped two fingers in as Ford held the jar. Logan's finger returned to my forbidden entry and worked the lubricant into me. Again and again they did that, ensuring I was slick and coated, inside and out. Not just one finger filled me, but two and I groaned as he nudged them deeper and deeper, all while Ford continued to fuck my pussy with first two fingers, then three.

When Logan was satisfied that I was ready, he nodded and they both removed their hands from my body.

I whimpered and swayed forward, Ford catching me by the shoulders and claiming my mouth with a soul-searing kiss as Logan settled on the bed with his back pressed to several pillows that were leaning against the headboard.

When Ford was finished kissing me, he swatted me on my bare bottom with a playful grin. "Get up there and give Logan a kiss."

Feeling like I was floating with happiness, I crawled to the head of the bed and kissed Logan, his touch and tongue taking me, exploring me with a gentle command that made me melt into him. I was ready to give my men anything. Everything.

When the kiss ended, Logan lifted his hands to my waist and flipped me around so I faced Ford, who now knelt between Logan's spread feet.

Ford moved forward, and Logan let go of my waist as Ford took over holding me in place. I knelt, my knees on either side of Logan's hips, his huge cock aligned with my tight rosette.

I looked at Ford as the tip of Logan's cock pressed to that entrance and I knew this was the moment I'd both wished for and feared.

I expected him to take my ass then, but he shifted, his hands on my hips pulled me down and he speared my pussy with one hard, fast strike.

I cried out at the penetration, but it wasn't enough. I lifted up, then lowered myself. With Logan's knees between mine, he spread my thighs, pushing me open making me go wider and wider as Logan grabbed my ankles. I couldn't move away. I couldn't close my legs. I could not escape.

"I need... it's... oh," I cried. My breasts bounced every time I lifted myself, then slammed down, hard on Logan's cock. Ford just held my thighs wide and watched, his cock turning an angry red as I watched. I was spread wide, but I longed for Ford's mouth on my clit, or his fingers, or his hand. "I need..."

"What do you need?" Ford asked.

"Touch me." I knew my response was not truly a request, and so did Ford.

"No. Not yet." He rose on his knees, grabbed me by the nape of my neck and kissed me, his tongue driving down into my mouth as Logan's cock thrust up into my pussy. They fucked me with cock and tongue, trapped between them, unable to find release. I was ready to explode. Felt like I was dying, on the verge of breaking into a thousand pieces.

The tear was a surprise, but I felt the hot, wet glide as it traveled down my cheek to hit Ford's palm where he held my face.

He lifted his head, breaking our kiss, and stared deep into my eyes as Logan thrust up into me, fucking me like the wild man I'd named him.

"What do you need, Lizzie?"

"You. I need both of you," I replied.

Ford looked behind me to Logan and gave a slight nod that nearly made me sob with relief.

Logan lifted me up all the way so his cock slipped free and I whimpered, aching and empty, desperate. Ford held out the jar again and this time, Logan used the lubricant on his cock, coating it liberally. Ford placed the jar back on the dresser and moved back, pulling me forward onto my hands and knees.

"Logan's going to go in slow, love."

He moved to kneel before me and he held my chin up, holding my gaze prisoner as Logan moved behind me.

Logan gripped my hips and pulled me toward him to settle me once again, this time with his very slick cock nudging at my back entrance. He loosened his hold on my hips and I pushed backward, trying to take him in. The broad head pressed inside, but not far. Ford's eyes flared and I heard Logan praising me, telling me how beautiful I was, how tight, how perfect. They'd trained me well, for while I winced at the stretching, it was not painful.

"Take him inside, Lizzie," Ford said. "Fill that virgin arse with his cock. I want to watch your face as he breaches that perfect hole."

I kept my eyes on Ford's as I shifted my hips and rocked backward, slowly trying to get Logan's huge cock in my bottom. Circling and shifting, pressing back and shifting some more, but I could not do it.

Sweat glistened on my skin and my nipples were hard as little pebbles.

"Breathe," Ford commanded. "Take a deep breath."

His dark eyes had me mesmerized and I couldn't look away. I did as he commanded and sucked in a lungful of air. Logan pressed forward, applying pressure that I hadn't felt before, forcing my body to accept him, to adjust to his huge size.

Ford nodded and leaned down to kiss me, once, twice. "Good girl. Now exhale and push down. More. More. Take his cock, Lizzie."

Ford reached beneath me and stroked my breasts, pulling on my nipples as he kissed me. Logan's huge cock was relentless, advancing in a slow assault that left me breathless and eager for more. All at once, Logan's flared head spread me wide. Something popped inside me as he breached that tight ring of muscle. I groaned at the thick feel of him and Logan cursed.

"Fuck!"

Ford didn't look away. "Ah, so beautiful. Now work him in. Nice and slowly. Take your time. Fuck him, Lizzie. Make him lose that iron control. Make sure he never forgets who he belongs to. Make him yours. Good girl. Such a good girl, taking Logan into that perfect ass."

"It's the tightest thing ever," Logan said, his voice rough.

"We're going to move you now, Lizzie." Ford pressed back on my shoulders as Logan pulled me toward him. One moment I was bent over, the next I was sitting on Logan's lap, my legs spread over his hips, his cock still deep inside.

His hands on my hips tightened, but he let me ride him at my own pace. I took more and more of him, working myself up and down his huge cock, just as if he were fucking my pussy, but so slow.

Logan's hands came up and he cupped my breasts once again, his lips kissing along the line of my shoulder. The feel of his fingers tweaking and playing with my nipples, tugging on them, had me relaxing and I took more and more of his cock into me. Soon enough, my thighs were resting against his and he was buried deep, his balls striking my bare bottom when I lowered myself all the way.

To say that I felt full was not true, for I knew that Ford was going to fuck my pussy too. At the same time. As if he could read my mind, Logan leaned back on his elbows and with his knees, nudged my thighs even wider.

When I thought I'd been open and exposed before, Logan wrapped his arms around my chest and pulled me back to lie down with my back pressed to his chest, his cock buried to the hilt in my ass, but my legs were spread wide, my pussy on display as if Logan were merely the bed I laid upon waiting for Ford to fuck me.

Ford moved between my legs, lining his cock up with my pussy. I felt the flared head slide over my pussy, then push against my dripping opening.

Ford leaned forward and our breaths mingled. "You're ours, love. While I may have taken your virginity and Logan just took that arse for the first time, this is it. This is our true joining. There's no going back. There's nothing between us now, and there never will be again."

His beard tickled my jaw as he whispered in my left ear.

Logan's thick voice whispered in my right, "The only thing between us, Lizzie, is you. Just like this. We're going to be one."

"Right now." Ford angled his hips and worked his cock in, filled me in one smooth stroke.

I cried out, a long keening sound. Two huge cocks filled me to the brim and I couldn't go anywhere. They had me trapped between them. I was pinned, controlled, held, filled, fucked. I was just where I wanted to be and I had no interest in escaping.

"You may come at any time and as often as you want." Logan's voice, his words had me so close to the edge already. This was the darkest, most carnal thing I'd ever done, ever imagined. It had been one thing to watch Emily with her husbands, but doing it, being fucked by two men who loved me, was something else entirely. They filled my body and my heart.

The men began to move then, alternating their strokes

and working my body. I couldn't even move, impaled as I was. I had to take whatever they gave me and it was *everything.*

"I love you, Lizzie," Logan whispered against my neck as he licked and sucked at the skin there. "Come all over me. Squeeze my cock."

"Come, love. Come now," Ford growled, his mouth roving over my shoulders, nipping at my lips as he fucked me.

I was gone, lost, filled, loved. I came, just as they commanded, because there was nothing else I could do but give them everything.

I screamed my release, every part of my body tingling and straining to take them harder, faster, deeper. The fucked me through it, their hard cocks pumping in and out, Logan's hand on my nipples pinching and pulling as Ford claimed my mouth. They pushed me to a second orgasm just seconds after the first.

They continued to fuck me as I floated in their arms, although it wasn't long at all before I felt Logan thrust deep and hold himself there, his body tensing under me as he pumped his seed into me as deep as it would go. He groaned and thrust again and again, then stilled. Ford soon followed, but I felt his seed hot and thick filling me, my body milking his cock to take as much of it as I could.

Ford breathed hard, as if he'd run a mile. Slowly, he pulled from me. "If we didn't make a baby out of this joining, we will before morning."

Taking my elbows, Ford helped me to lift up and off Logan's cock. As I knelt between them, I looked down and watched their seed slide from me. It trickled down my thighs and dripped onto the bedding.

My body felt used and stretched and swollen, my legs wobbly and my body sated and well satisfied. But one word rang in my thoughts like a bell.

"Baby?" I asked.

Logan stroked my back, his gentle touch lulling me to lean into him. "You do know how babies are made?" he asked. I glanced back at him over my shoulder in time to catch his wicked grin.

I couldn't help but smile back. "I do, but I don't think it works if your seed is in my bottom."

Ford waggled his eyebrows as he moved to lie down in the center of the bed. "Then Logan should get cleaned up, for it is his turn to fill that sweet pussy."

I was tugged into Ford's embrace, his hard cock ready to take me again. Just a few moments later, Logan returned from the washbasin, ready to go again, ready to plant his seed in my pussy so we could have a baby.

A baby!

I was ready for my husbands to take me again, to fill me up, for I knew I had found my true home with these two men. With two husbands, I would always be well fucked, certainly, but well loved, too.

FIND YOUR MATCH!

Do you love Grace Goodwin's Interstellar Brides® Program? Now it's your turn! YOUR mate is out there. Take the test today and discover your perfect match. Are you ready for a sexy alien mate (or two)?

VOLUNTEER NOW!
interstellarbridesprogram.com

WANT MORE?

Sign up for Grace's VIP Reader list at
http://freescifiromance.com

Have you the Bestselling Interstellar Brides® Program? Don't miss out on the fun. Read the first chapter of MASTERED BY HER MATES (The FREE prequel) below:

Amanda Bryant, Interstellar Brides Processing Center, Earth

This couldn't be real. But it *felt* real. The warm air on my sweaty skin. The redolent scent of fucking. The soft sheets beneath my knees. The hard body at my back. I was blindfolded, the silk making everything as black as night.

But I didn't need sight to know a cock was buried deep in my pussy. A big, thick cock.

It was real. *It was real!*

I was kneeling on a bed, the man behind me, fucking me. His hips shifted, rocking his cock over every delicious nerve ending, my inner walls rippling around him. His hard thighs were beneath me, an arm wrapped about my waist and cupping my breast, anchoring me in place so I couldn't move. I could only take it as he bottomed out deep inside me. I could go nowhere—not that I wished to. Why would I want to leave? It felt *so* good. *His cock* felt so good stretching me open, filling me.

It wasn't just the man behind me making me lose my mind. A second man—yes, I was with two men!—kissed his way down my belly. Hot licks of his tongue in my navel, then lower and lower…

How long could he take for his lips to finish their journey to my clit?

That little nub pulsed and throbbed in eagerness. Hurry, tongue, hurry!

How could this be real? How could two men be touching me, licking me, fucking me? They were. Because the man at my back wrapped his strong hands around my inner thighs and opened me even wider for the other to explore me with his hands and tongue…and found my clit.

Finally! I rocked my hips forward, wanting more.

"Hold still, mate. We know you want to come, but you will wait." The deep voice at my ear breathed the heated words against the side of my neck, even as he shifted his hips, spreading me open with his giant cock.

Wait? I couldn't wait! Every time the cock plunged deep, the tongue on my clit flicked, then licked. No woman could survive a cock plus a flick and lick.

I moaned. Whimpered, tried to circle my hips into the pleasure. I loved it. I wanted them both inside me. Was desperate for them to claim me, to make me theirs forever.

For a split second my mind rebelled, as I had no mates. I hadn't taken a lover in over a year. I'd never taken two men at once. Never considered wanting both of my holes filled. Who were these men? Why was I—

The tongue was gone from my clit and I cried out. "No!"

Soon, that mouth was on my nipple, and I felt the man before me smile against my tender skin. He tugged and suckled me until I whimpered, begging for more. I rode the razor's edge, my body on the brink of orgasm. The cock filling me was incredible, but it wasn't enough.

I needed.

"More."

The plea left my lips before I could regain control and a dark part of me thrilled at the punishment I knew the demand would bring. How did I know that? I was so confused, but didn't want to take any time to think, just enjoy.

Immediately, a strong hand wrapped in my hair, tugging my head back with a painful sting as the man behind me twisted my head to his, teasing my lips with his own.

"You do not make demands, mate. You submit." He kissed me, his tongue a hard, dominant intrusion in my mouth. He thrust as he fucked me, his tongue and his cock invading my body as one before withdrawing to the edge and plunging within once more.

My other mate—wait, mate?—used his fingers to spread my pussy lips even wider. He licked my clit, then blew on it gently as the cock fucking me slammed deep, then pulled nearly free. Lick. Blow. Lick. Blow. I was near tears, my arousal too intense to be contained.

"Please, please. *Please.*"

A single tear fell and escaped the edges of my blind-fold, wetting the skin where my cheek and my mate's touched. He broke the kiss instantly, his warm tongue tracing the path with a loud rumble. "Ah begging. We love our mate to beg. That means you are ready."

The one I imagined must be on his knees before me, the one torturing me with his mouth, spoke to me then.

"Do you accept my claim, mate? Do you give yourself to me and my second freely, or do you wish to choose another primary male?"

"I accept your claim, warriors." My vow spoken, my mates growled, their control pushed to its limit.

"Then we claim you in the rite of naming. You belong to us and we shall kill any other warrior who dares to touch you."

"May the gods witness and protect you." The chorus of voices sounded around us and I gasped as the man on his knees before me nipped at my inner thighs with his teeth in a dark promise of more pleasure.

"Come for us now, mate. Show them all how your mates bring you pleasure." The mate at my back issued the order just before his mouth crushed my lips in a searing kiss.

Wait, what others?—Before I could finish the thought the other man's mouth clamped down, hard on my clit, sucking and flicking his tongue, pushing me over the edge.

I screamed, but the sound was lost to me as waves of ecstasy crashed through me. My body became taut like a bow, only my pussy walls rippled and clenched the cock that continued to fuck me. Hard, so hard and yet the tongue that continued to flick my clit was so soft and gentle.

Heat bloomed on my skin, bright white flickered behind my eyelids, my fingers tingled. Hell, my entire body tingled. But my mates weren't finished with me, they did not allow me to catch my breath before I was lifted off the large cock and turned around. I heard the rustle of sheets, felt the bed shift, then I was lifted on top of him. With hands on my hips, I was lowered back onto his cock. In seconds, he had filled me again, pumping up into me as my other mate reached around between us and fingered my clit. I was so primed, so sensitive, that I was instantly on edge.

Desire spiraled within, and I tensed, holding my breath as fire rushed through me. I was going to come again. They worked me so simply, yet they knew my body, knew how to touch me, how to lick and suck me. How to fuck me so perfectly that all I could do was come. Again and again. "Yes. Yes. Yes!"

"No."

The command was like a leash and my orgasm came to

heel, waiting. A firm hand spanked my bare bottom. The sound of it was a loud crack, the feel of it a bright flash of pain. Three times. Four. When he stopped, the prickly heat of it spread through me. I *should* have hated it. He'd spanked me! But no. My traitorous body *liked* it, for the extra sensation went straight to my breasts, my clit. My whole body felt like it was on fire and I wanted more. I wanted their commands. I wanted their control. I wanted it all. I *needed* both of my mates to fill me, to fuck me, to claim me. I wanted to be theirs forever.

Firm hands locked onto my ass, pulling my cheeks open for the mate behind me. Even as the one lying beneath me held me open, he ground his pelvis, fucking me with small strokes into a blissful euphoria. My pussy was stuffed so full, how could my other mate fit in my ass? How could the two of them claim me properly without causing me pain? Somehow I knew that I would like it. Memories of a large plug filling me, spreading me open, getting me ready for this, reassured me. I'd liked the plug filling me as they fucked me, so I would surely die of pleasure when I had two cocks in me.

The need wasn't just to fuck both of my mates at once. It was to stake my claim and make these men mine forever. Only their double penetration would do it. I *loved* these men. I wanted them. I wanted them both.

My mate's finger explored my tight ass, a virgin to a cock, but I knew he would fit. Both men were powerful and dominant, and yet gentle. The mating oil he used to work one finger inside, then another, was a welcome heat in my body. I panted as the warmth of his fingers slowly spread me open, ensuring I was truly ready to be claimed.

Arms wrapped around my back and the mate beneath me pulled me down so I rested on his broad chest. His hand stroked up and down the length of my spine.

"Arch your back. Yes, like that." The fingers slipped from my ass and while I felt open and ready, I felt empty. I *needed* more. The mate behind me continued. "When I get my cock into this snug little ass, you will be ours forever. You are the link, connecting us as one."

The blunt head of his cock pressed forward, slowly, filling me until I thought I would die from pleasure. The pre-cum on the tip of his cock slipped inside me and made fire spread through my nerve endings, like a jolt of electricity that went straight to my clit.

I tried to hold on, I tried to behave, to deny the pleasure spiraling through me, to wait for permission, but I could not.

I came with a scream, my pussy convulsing so hard I nearly forced the second cock from my body with the force of the muscle spasms. I couldn't think, couldn't breathe, and each thrust of my mates' cocks pushed me higher, until I came again—

"Yes!"

"Miss Bryant."

The woman's voice seemed to appear out of thin air, filling my mind with the cold chill of reality. I ignored it, reaching for the ecstasy I'd just experienced, but the more I tried to focus on my mates, the harder it became to feel them. Their scent was gone. Their heat, gone. Their cocks, gone. I cried out a denial as hard, cold fingers wrapped around my shoulder, shaking me.

"Miss Bryant!"

No one touched me like that. No one.

Years of martial arts training kicked in and I tried to swing my arm to block the assault on my shoulder. I did not want those cold hands touching me. I didn't want anyone touching me, anyone but my mates. Those strong hands that were so gentle.

The sharp pain of restraints cutting into my wrists brought me back to reality. I couldn't knock the hand away, I couldn't punch her. I was trapped. Restrained. Cuffed to some kind of chair. Defenseless.

Blinking, I looked around, trying to regain my bearings. God, my pussy was pulsing with desire and my breathing was ragged. I was naked beneath some type of hospital gown, cuffed to an exam table that looked more like a dentist's chair than a hospital bed. Air whooshed in and out of my lungs in rapid panting sounds as I tried to calm my racing heart. My engorged clit throbbed. I wanted to touch it with my fingers, to finish what the men had started, but that was impossible. In the restraints, all I could do was grip my hands into fists.

I'd had an orgasm, right here in this damn chair, pinned and naked like a freak. I was a five-year intelligence operative. I'd been assigned this mission because my country was trusting me to maintain control, to do what needed to be done out there in space. Not fall apart and beg for orgasms from the first alien whose hard cock made me so hot I forgot my own name.

I recognized the signs and knew my face was turning a dark shade of pink at the thought of not just *one* dominant, commanding alpha male making my pussy weep, making me beg. One lover? A hint of normalcy? No. Not me. I had to make things interesting and imagine fucking two of them at the same time. God, my mother would be rolling over in her grave right now.

"Miss Bryant?" There was that voice again.

"Yes." Resigned, I turned my head to find a group of seven women watching me with obvious curiosity. They all wore dark gray uniforms with a strange burgundy insignia over their left breasts. I'd seen that symbol often enough the last two months, it was the mark of the Interstellar Coalition, indicating they were all employees of the Interstellar Bride Program's testing center, Wardens, they were called, as if signing with the Coalition were a jail sentence. The women were a cross-section of races, black, white, Asian, Hispanic. They represented all the races of Earth. How fucking perfect. A pale-skinned woman with dark brown hair and sympathetic gray eyes was the one speaking to me. I knew her name, but she didn't know that. I knew a lot of things I wasn't supposed to know.

I licked my lips, swallowed. "I'm awake."

My voice was scratchy as if I'd been crying out. Oh God. Had I really screamed when I came? Had I begged and moaned as these stoic women bore witness?

"Excellent." The Warden looked like she was in her late twenties, perhaps a year or two younger than me. "I am Warden Egara, and I am in charge of the Interstellar Bride Program here on Earth. The processing program indicates a successful match has been made for you, but since you are the first volunteer bride that's been matched using the Interstellar Bride protocols, we will need to ask you a few additional questions."

"Okay." I took a deep breath, let it out. The desire was

slowly seeping away, the sweat on my skin gone. Goose bumps rose on my flesh in the cool, air-conditioned room that worked so hard to stave off the heat of Miami in August. The hard chair felt sticky and the gown scratchy against my sensitive skin. Leaning my head back, I waited.

According to the aliens promising to "protect" the Earth from an alleged threat known as the Hive, these human women who stood before me had been mated to alien warriors in the past, and were now widows who had volunteered to serve the Coalition here on Earth.

Oh, and there were more than two-hundred and sixty alien races fighting in the Coalition forces, but they claimed only a fraction were compatible for mating with humans. That seemed odd. And how did they know, if a human had never been sent to space before?

The Coalition ships had shown up a couple months ago, on a Wednesday, June 4 at 6:53 p.m. Eastern Time. Yes, I remember the time exactly, like I'd forget the moment when I found out there really were others "out there". I'd been hitting the treadmill at the gym, twenty-three minutes into my ninety-minute workout when the television screens lining the walls had all gone crazy. Every channel was suddenly alien ships, alien landings all over the world, and fucking huge, seven-foot tall, yellow alien warriors in black camo armor walking off their little shuttles like they owned us already.

Whatever. They spoke our languages and claimed to have just won a battle in our solar system. Once they had a television crew in their face, they demanded a meeting with every major world leader. A few days later, at that meeting in Paris, the aliens had refused to acknowledge the sovereignty of any country and demanded Earth choose one supreme leader, a Prime, they called it. One representative for the entire world. Countries were irrelevant. Our laws? Irrelevant. We were part of their Coalition now, and must follow their laws.

That meeting had been broadcast live all over the world in every major language, not by our television stations on Earth, but by their control of our satellite network. Angry and terrified world leaders broadcast live on international television in every country?

Let's just say, the meeting had not gone well.

My blood boiled as I watched. Riots erupted. People were scared. The President had called out the National Guard and every police force and fire department in the country had been working overtime for two weeks. That was about how long it took people to realize the aliens weren't going to just blow us up and take what they wanted.

But then...this. Brides. Soldiers. They said they didn't want our planet, claimed to be protecting us, but they wanted our soldiers to fight in their war and human women mated to their warriors. And I was the crazy bitch who'd volunteered to be the first human sacrifice.

Giant, yellow alien sex? Because that's what brides did, have sex with their mate. Yeah, it wasn't a *husband* but a *mate*. Coming right up.

Yay, me.

The sarcastic thought made me shiver and I shook my head to clear it. I was on a mission, a critical assignment. The thought of fucking one of those huge warriors with a massive chest, golden skin and dominant expression should not excite me. I didn't know who I'd get, but from all of the TV footage, they were *all* big. They were *all* dominant.

But it did excite me and I hoped that I'd find at least some pleasure in this mission. If I didn't, I would endure. But if I could ride one of their huge cocks to a mind-numbing orgasm once in a while, would that be so bad? I'd consider it a perk of the job. I was giving up my life, my home, my whole fucking planet for the next few years. A couple of decent orgasms shouldn't be too much to ask. Right?

I'd spent years serving my country, and I was confident in my ability to handle any situation, adapt to anything. I was a survivor, and more, I wasn't buying their story, and neither had my superiors at the agency. Where was the proof? Where were these horrible Hive creatures?

The Coalition commanders showed videos to our leaders that any junior high kid with the right software could have created. No one on Earth had ever seen a Hive soldier in the flesh, and the Coalition commanders refused to give us the weapons and technology we would need to defend ourselves from such a deadly threat.

Me? I'd always been a skeptic, and extremely pragmatic. If something needed to be done to protect my country, I did it. I'd been worried about the usual, terrorism, global warming, illegal arms dealers, drug smuggling, international hacker taking control of our energy or banking systems. And now? Aliens. I still couldn't quite wrap my head around that, despite the fact that I'd watched hours of videos and interviews with their huge, golden commanders from a planet called Prillon Prime. Seven foot of sexy on a stick.

So...one. I'd seen *one* race of aliens, out of the supposed hundreds. Even their processing center people, these Wardens, were humans they'd most likely brainwashed.

For a first contact scenario, the Prillon warriors weren't doing much convincing. One would think they would have a better propaganda strategy going. Either that, or they didn't give a shit what we thought because they were actually telling the truth and a very aggressive, nasty race of aliens along the lines of the Borg from *Star Trek* was waiting in the wings to destroy all life on Earth.

I was going with theory number one, but we couldn't eliminate the possibility of theory number two. Earth did not want to be *assimilated.*

My job? To find out the truth. And the only way anyone was going to do that was actually to go out into space. They weren't taking soldiers yet, so lucky me, I was going the other route. The Interstellar Bride Program.

This was not how I'd envisioned my big day. No, I'd wanted the usual, a ridiculously expensive white dress, flowers, corny music played on harps and a bunch of family members in the pews I was paying a fortune to feed but that I hadn't seen in a decade.

Speaking of weddings, how the hell had the women standing before me supposedly been mated to aliens, when, until a couple of months ago, humanity hadn't even known that aliens existed?

"How do you feel?" Warden Egara asked, and I realized I'd probably been staring off into space for a few minutes as my thoughts chased each other in circles inside my head.

"Feel?" I repeated.

Really? I took a moment to take stock of my body. My pussy was dripping wet and the gown scrunched up beneath me was soaked. My clit throbbed in time with my pulse, and I'd just had two of the most incredible orgasms of my life. Good day to be a spy.

"As you're well aware, you are the first human woman to volunteer for the Interstellar Bride Program, so we're curious as to how you experienced the processing."

"I'm your guinea pig?"

They all smiled, but it seemed only Warden Egara had been elected to speak. "In a sense, yes. Please tell us how you feel after your testing."

"I feel fine."

My gaze raked over their earnest expressions, but the one woman, the one with the dark hair who'd woken me from the dream, Warden Egara, cleared her throat.

"During the, um, simulation—"

Ah, so that's what they were calling it.

"—did you experience the dream as a third-party witness? Or did it feel like you were really, you know, there?"

I sighed. What else could I do? I *felt* like I'd just had mind-blowing monkey sex with two huge alien warriors...and I'd loved it. "I was there. It was all happening to me."

"So, you felt like you were the bride? That your mate was claiming you?"

174

Claiming? That was *way* more than just claiming. That was…wow.

"Mates. And yes." Crap. Heat ran up my neck to pink my cheeks again. Mates? As in two. Now, why had I admitted to that?

The Warden Egara's shoulders relaxed. "Two mates? Correct?"

"That's what I said."

She clapped her hands together and I turned to see a look of happy relief on her face. "Excellent! You were matched to Prillon Prime, so everything appears to be working perfectly."

Big golden warrior for me, just like the ones on TV? Check. And how convenient that I wasn't matched to one of the *other* races. I truly had to wonder if the others even existed.

The Warden turned to one of the other women. "Warden Gomes, will you please inform the Coalition that the protocol has been integrated into the human population and appears to be fully functional. We should be able to process volunteer brides at all seven centers within a few weeks."

"Of course, Warden Egara. It will be my pleasure," Warden Gomes replied, her response thick with a Portuguese accent. "I am eager to return to Rio, to see my family."

Warden Egara sighed happily and walked away from me to lift a tablet monitor from the table on the edge of the room before returning to me. "All right. Since you're the first woman in the Interstellar Bride Program, I hope you'll be patient as we work through the protocols."

She smiled, and the look on her face was radiant, as if she were thrilled to be sending me off planet to be married to an alien I'd never met. Had all these women *really* been married to aliens? Why were they the ones asking questions? I wanted to know more. Up until a couple months ago, aliens were only little green men in movies, or disgusting things with tentacles that either hunted us, or deposited larvae that made our chest explode.

Ugh. I watched too many sci-fi movies. And now that I was totally creeped out, I decided now was a good time to stall. "Um… I need to talk to my father before we go any further. He will be worried."

"Oh, of course!" She stepped back and lowered the tablet, holding it at her side. "You should say your good-byes, Amanda. Once we begin the protocol, you'll be processed and transported immediately."

"Today? Now?" Oh crap. I wasn't ready for *now*.

She nodded. "Yes. Now. I'll go get your family." She left me alone, the other women streaming out in a line behind her. I stared at the ceiling, clenching and unclenching my fists, trying to remain calm.

My father? Yeah, so not true. He wasn't my family, but the Warden didn't know that. I hadn't been home to New York in two months. Home? It was more of an apartment where I slept when I was not on assignment. Which was… practically never. But hey, at least I wouldn't miss it.

My boss had called me in during my only three days off in the last three months, flown me straight from New York to the Pentagon for two months of intense debriefing and preparation. When I'd landed in Miami, they'd picked me up in a limousine. I should have known I'd wouldn't go home again before the processing occurred. Hell, I *had* known, but some poor little corner of my heart had still been hoping this was all some big fucking joke.

No such luck, and there wasn't anything I could do about it. It wasn't like you could tell the Company no. My job wasn't the kind where you could just quit. It wasn't the Mafia, but a spy didn't just resign and become a school teacher either. There was *always* a new assignment. A job. A new threat, a new enemy.

But sending me out into space as an alien bride? That was off the charts, even for them. Still, I knew why I'd been chosen. I spoke five languages fluently, had been an active field agent for five years, and more importantly, I was single, with no family ties and nothing to lose. My parents were dead and I was a woman. Seemed the aliens only requested female brides, and I wondered if any of them were gay? Did the gay warriors request brides? Or did they just hook up with their fellow warriors and call it good?

So many questions without answers. That's why they needed me.

Guinea pig? Sacrificial lamb? Yep. That about summed it up.

The heavy door swung open and my boss walked in, followed by a man I recognized, but barely knew. They both wore plain blue suits, white button-down shirts, one yellow and one paisley tie. Their hair was graying at the temples, both styles military short. They were unremarkable, men you'd walk past on a busy sidewalk and never take note of, unless you looked in their eyes. They were two of the most dangerous men I knew, and I knew quite a few in my line of work. They'd been chosen by the President to do whatever needed to be done to ascertain the truth about this new alien threat.

Apparently I wasn't the only one who wasn't buying the —*we're here to save you, just give us your soldiers and your women*—line of bullshit these aliens were spewing. Not one government on Earth was happy and the U.S. and her allies were determined to discover the truth. And, with my mixed heritage of an Irish father and half black, half Asian mother, they'd all agreed I represented a whole lot of humanity. They'd requested I volunteer for this assignment.

Lucky me.

"Amanda."

"Robert." I nodded at the silent man to his right and had no idea if I even knew his real name. "Allen."

Robert cleared his throat. "How did the processing go?"

"Fine. Warden Egara says I've been matched to Prillon Prime."

Allen nodded. "Excellent. The Prillon warriors are in command of the entire Coalition Fleet. We were also informed that they keep their brides with them on their battleships, on the front lines of this alleged war. You should have access to weapons, tactical information and their most advanced technologies."

Great. Two weeks ago, when I had agreed to take this mission, I would have been thrilled. But now? My heart beat a little too fast at the idea that what I really *wanted* was unlimited access to two smoking-hot, dominant alien warriors' bodies…

Robert crossed his arms over his chest and glared down at me, trying to put on his protective father-figure face. I'd seen through that act years ago, but I played along as he continued. "While the Bride Program appears to be up and running, they are not yet ready to begin processing our soldiers for their military. They won't complete testing over there for a few more days. Once they do, we'll send two of our men along to infiltrate the unit and assist with your mission. The men have already been selected. They're good men, Amanda. Completely black."

"Understood." And I did. Black, as in special operations assets so critical to national security that they didn't officially exist. They were sending super soldiers to cover all their bases. Me in the enemy's bed, the soldiers in their military units.

"One way or another, find out the true extent of the Hive threat to Earth, send back weapons and engineering schematics from their ships, and anything else you can get our hands on." I knew my orders, but Robert didn't hesitate to repeat them one last time.

The aliens had magnanimously offered Earth protection from the Hive, but repeatedly refused to share their advanced weaponry or transporter technology with Earth. Earth's governments were not pleased. Nothing like being on top of the world, a superpower for decades, then being sent with your tail between your legs to the back of the bus. There wasn't just *us* anymore, humans. It was an entire universe of planets and races and cultures and...enemies.

Robert lifted his arm to squeeze my shoulder. "We're counting on you. The whole world is counting on you."

"I know, sir." No pressure, right? "I won't let you down."

Warden Egara chose that moment to return, her bright smile and cheery demeanor brittle and a little too shiny. I wasn't sure what she thought of my two visitors, but whatever it was, she wasn't pleased.

"So, are you ready, Miss Bryant?"

"Yes."

"If you'll excuse us, gentlemen?" When the two suits were gone she turned to me, the tablet in her lap and her smile genuine. "You okay? I know it can be tough leaving your family."

She looked over her shoulder at the closed door, and I realized she was referring to Robert, my supposed father.

"Oh, um...yeah. I'm fine. We're not that...close."

The warden studied me intently for a moment, must have seen I had no emotional ties, and continued. "Okay. So, to begin the protocol—for the record, state your name, please."

"Amanda Bryant."

"Miss Bryant, are you now, or have you ever been married?"

"No." Engaged once, but that had ended the night I told my fiancé what I did for a living. I wasn't supposed to tell him I was a spy, so bad on me...

"Do you have any biological offspring?"

"No."

She tapped her screen a few times without looking at me. "I am required to inform you, Miss Bryant, that you will have thirty days to accept or reject the mate chosen for you by the Interstellar Bride Program's matching protocols."

"Okay. And what if I reject the match? What happens? Will I be sent back to Earth?"

"Oh no. There will be no return to Earth. As of this moment, you are no longer a citizen of Earth."

"Wait. What?" I did not like the sound of that. Never come back? Ever? I'd figured a year or two in the field and I'd come home, retire on a sandy beach and sip piña coladas for a few years. Now I couldn't come home? My citizenship revoked? Could they even *do* that?

Suddenly I was shaking, and not with excitement or arousal, with dread. No one at the office said I wouldn't be coming back. They had to have known. God, after five years of service, they were just sending me to outer space as what…some kind of noble sacrifice? Those assholes at the agency had conveniently forgotten to mention this one, small detail.

"You, Miss Bryant, are now a warrior bride of Prillon Prime, subject to that planet's laws, customs and protections. If your mate is unacceptable, you may request a new primary mate after thirty days. You may continue the mating process, on Prillon Prime, until you find a mate who *is* acceptable."

I tugged at the restraints on the table, my mind racing a thousand miles an hour. Could I escape? Could I change my mind? Forever? Never come home? The reality of leaving Earth behind forever pressed in on my chest until I couldn't get enough air. The room started spinning.

"Miss Bryant— Oh, dear." Warden Egara's hand flew over her tablet for a few seconds before she put it down on the table behind her. "You'll be fine, love. I promise."

Promise? She'd promise that I was going to be fine with being transported into outer space and never...ever coming home?

The wall behind me lit with a strange blue light and the chair beneath me jolted a bit as it began to move sideways, toward the light.

I couldn't look. Instead, I closed my eyes and focused on filling my lungs with fresh air. I didn't panic. Ever. This was so unlike me.

But then, I'd never had multiple orgasms in a damn testing chair either. And I'd never, ever fantasized about taking two lovers at once. The way they'd made me feel had been like nothing I'd ever felt on Earth. Would it be like that? Would my men make me feel that way?

The warden's warm fingers wrapped around my wrist gently and I opened my eyes to find her concerned face hovering nearby. She smiled at me, like a preschool teacher smiling at a scared four-year-old on the first day of class.

"Don't worry so much. The match was ninety-nine percent. Your mate will be perfect for you, and you for him. The system works. When you wake up, you'll be with your mate. He will take care of you. You're going to be happy, Amanda. I promise."

"But—"

"When you wake, Amanda Bryant, your body will have

been prepared for Prillon Prime's matching customs and your mate's requirements. He will be waiting for you." Her voice had become more formal, as if she recited another protocol by rote.

"Wait—I," My voice stalled as two large metallic arms with gigantic needles on the ends appeared to be headed for the sides of my face. "What is that?" I knew I sounded panicked, couldn't help it. I did not do needles.

"Don't worry, dear, they will insert the Neuroprocessing Units that will integrate with the language centers of your brain, allowing you to speak and understand any language."

Okay. Holy shit, I guess I was about to be implanted with some of their advanced technology. I held completely still as the two needles pierced the sides of my temples, just above my ears.

If all else failed, I could come home and Robert could cut the damn chips, or whatever they were, out of my head. Sad thing was, I knew he'd do it.

But what if I never came back? What if the aliens were telling the truth? What if I fell in love with my mate…?

My chair slipped inside a small enclosure and I was lowered, chair and all, into a warm, soothing tub of strange blue water. "Your processing will being in three…two…one."

Read more now!

DO YOU LOVE AUDIOBOOKS?

Grace Goodwin's books are now available as
audiobooks...everywhere.

CONNECT WITH GRACE

Interested in joining my not-so-secret Facebook Sci-Fi Squad? Get excerpts, cover reveals and sneak peeks before anyone else. Be part of a closed Facebook group that shares pictures and fun news. JOIN Here: http://bit.ly/SciFiSquad

All of Grace's books can be read as sexy, stand-alone adventures. Her Happily-Ever-Afters are always free from cheating because she writes Alpha males, NOT Alpha-holes. (You can figure that one out.) But be careful...she likes her heroes hot and her love scenes hotter. You have been warned...

www.gracegoodwin.com
gracegoodwinauthor@gmail.com

ABOUT GRACE

Grace Goodwin is a *USA Today* and international best-selling author of Sci-Fi & Paranormal romance. Grace believes all women should be treated like princesses, in the bedroom and out of it, and writes love stories where men know how to make their women feel pampered, protected and very well taken care of. Grace hates the snow, loves the mountains (yes, that's a problem) and wishes she could simply download the stories out of her head instead of being forced to type them out. Grace lives in the western US and is a full-time writer, an avid romance reader and an admitted caffeine addict.

Made in the USA
Las Vegas, NV
20 January 2021